Initiations:
A Selection of Young Native Writings

Copyright © 2007 The Authors

Library and Archives Canada Cataloguing in Publication

Initiations : a selection of young Native writings / by Marilyn Dumont ... [et al.].

ISBN 978-1-894778-47-3

1. Canadian literature (English)--Native authors. 2. Native youth--Canada--Literary collections. 3. Canadian literature (English)--21st century. 4. Teenagers' writings, Canadian (English). I. Dumont, Marilyn

PS8235.I6I55 2007   C810.8'09283   C2007-905405-6

Published by Theytus Books
Penticton, B.C.

Printed and bound in Canada
on 100% post consumer fibre paper (100% recycled),
FSC and ancient forest friendly paper.

On behalf on Theytus Books, we would like to acknowledge the support of the following:
We acknowledge the financial support of the Government of Canada through the Book Publishing Industry Development Program (BPIDP) for our publishing activities.
We acknowledge the support of the Canada Council for the Arts which last year invested $20.1 million in writing and publishing throughout Canada.
Nous remercions de son soutien le Conseil des Arts du Canada, qui a investi 20,1 millions de dollars l'an dernier dans les lettres et l'édition à travers le Canada.
We acknowledge the support of the Province of British Columbia through the British Columbia Arts Council.

Initiations:

A Selection of Young Native Writings

Edited by Marilyn Dumont

Table of Contents

Preface *by Marilyn Dumont* .... *vii*

Erased *by Kelsea Northrop Donovan* *1*

Land Warmed by the Sun *by Denise Marie Williams* *5*

Makya *by Trisha Redman* *9*

The Power of One and All *by Kyle G. Wilson* *15*

Election Day *by Cory Cappo* *20*

My Brother Lonnie *by Chantelle Cheekinew* *26*

My Lesson *by Caitlyn Therrien* *33*

Occupied *by Joe Restoule General* *36*

STEH-WAH *by Kerissa M. Dickie* *40*

Going the Distance *by Sara General* *46*

Across the Barricade *by Alicia Elliott* *52*

Good Child *by Tony Liske* *57*

A Day of Healing *by Nicholas Printup* *61*

Echoes of Tamarack *by Candace Brunette* *65*

Wild Flowers *by Kerissa M. Dickie* *67*

Silence Speaks a Thousand Words *by Amanda Wapass-Griffin* *73*

The Enchanted Owl *by Jessica Yarrow* *79*

Remember, My Grandson, Remember Us *by Nicole Munro* *83*

Maternal Ties *by Sable Sweetgrass* *87*

The Unknown *by Réal Carrière* *92*

Translations *97*

Writer Biographies *98*

Preface

INITIATIONS is a collection of creative writing by Aboriginal youth in Canada and is a partnership of The Dominion Institute and Theytus Books. The stories were gathered over three years of the Aboriginal Writing Challenge; a national writing contest, which is also known as the Our Story Challenge, initiated by the Dominion Institute in 2005.

The challenge posed to aboriginal youth was to write a narrative that portrayed a moment or period in Aboriginal history. The top ten stories each year in two age categories (14-18 and 19-29) were awarded prizes based on their "creativity and originality."

Here is a selection of stories that I gravitate to because of their poetic language; their attention to beauty in the sounds they use to release their story, and their attention to the impulse to invest themselves in their words. There's poetry here, there's poetic prose, there's fiction and non-fiction, there's biography, there's personal essay and there's song. If I sing its praises, it's because I have known these stories longer and because they are all from aboriginal youth living in Canada...

Marilyn Dumont

ERASED
by Kelsea Northrop Donovan

A warm breeze touched Nita's face as she looked up to gaze at the warm sun that hung high in the sky like a ripe orange waiting to be picked. Nita smiled; the smell of Mama's cooking drifted through the air. Nita inhaled, breathing deeply. Suddenly, a strong chemical smell filled her nose. The sun disappeared, the sky turned black, and thick, dark rain clouds covered the beautiful orange sun. Nita ran towards the cabin and pushed open the door. "Mama, Mama, the sun is gone! Mama?" Nita cried turning round and round searching for her mother. Then, cold pale hands grabbed her; they began scrubbing, and scrubbing. Soap slid down her face and into her eyes. Her eyes burned, tears streamed down her face. Nita screamed.

Nita sat up straight in bed and gasped for air. Nightmares had haunted her sleep since coming to the school. Nita rocked slowly, and rubbed her hands up and down her arms. She looked sideways and saw the sleeping forms of her roommates. Nita breathed a sigh of longing. She wished that the hard cot she was sitting on was her wooden bed and quilt at home. She pushed away the longing feeling, and rolled over and pulled her grey blanket to her chin and closed her eyes.

The pale sun streamed through the tiny windows and landed on Nita's face. She stretched her arms high over her head and let out a loud yawn. She looked over to the other side of the room and saw her roommates making their beds frantically. Nita blinked and then remembered. She shot out of bed as if she had sat on a bed of thorns. She quickly brought the edges of the thin grey blanket together and folded them neatly at the edge of the cot.

A loud knock startled the girls. Sister Agnes stepped into the room and smelled the air. She frowned and crinkled her nose. She strolled over to Nita's bed and examined the messily folded bed sheets. She crinkled her nose again.

"Pupil 23, your bed is not in order, come over here," she ordered.

Nervous, Nita walked over and approached slowly as if Sister Agnes was an aggravated black bear. Sister pulled the strap from her back dress pocket.

"Lay out your hand," she barked.

Nita held out her hand cautiously and held it close to her body. Sister raised the strap and brought it down quickly on top of Nita's hand. A sharp pain weaned through Nita's hand, quickly spreading from her palm to her fingertips. The nun looked down at her, her thin blonde eyebrows raised in question. Nita frowned but she refused to cry. Sister Agnes scowled and then moved on to inspect the other girls' beds. Nita looked at her right hand. Her palm was bright red and a massive welt formed its way across her palm. Nita blew on her hand, to try to cool the heat of the throbbing.

Memories of the first day filled her head. She remembered feeling alone even though the halls had been full of girls struggling to get to class on time. Some of the girls chatted to their friends in English, quietly. Nita recalled not being able to then speak the *fish language*, or "English" as the Sisters called it. Nita called it the *fish language*; the way the Sisters' mouths opened and closed reminded Nita of fishing with Papa, and pulling the fish onto land where all it could do was open and close its wide mouth.

Somebody bumped Nita's shoulder causing her to drop her books. The banging of the books on the floor pulled Nita out of her thoughts and back into the clinical hallways of the school. The halls were still somewhat full of girls as Nita kneeled down, grabbed her books and walked briskly to class. She entered the classroom and sat in the back in her usual seat. She hated English class and wished it were mathematics as this was Nita's favourite subject. English bored her to the point of insanity. Nita put her books into a prim pile and lined up her pencil alongside it. Sister Katherine walked steadily between the desks and handed out the worksheet they would be working on. Nita stared down at the white paper in front of her. It reminded her of how everything here was: bland, boring, and pale. Nita brought her pencil to the page and wrote her name at the top of the page. She paused and looked at the paper. She had written Nita at the top of her paper. She then began to erase her name. As the eraser rubbed away her name, she felt a part of herself being rubbed away with it. Nita wrote the number 23 at the top of her paper. Now there was no Nita, there was only a number; her name had been reduced to a number. Nita glared at the paper now; it seemed to challenge her entire being. She wanted to shred that white paper to bits, and scream as she did it. Nita had been so occupied with her paper that she hadn't even realized someone new had entered the room. Nita looked up from her paper; Sister Katherine was frowning at a paper an older pupil had given to her.

"Pupil 23, listen next time you are called. You are excused from class and are to go see Sister Diane," barked Sister Agnes.

Nita rose slowly, gathered her books and her pencil, and walked slowly between the desks. The girls peered at her; they whispered quietly and were quickly shushed by Sister Katherine.

Nita exited the classroom and walked quickly to Sister Diane's office. Sister Diane was the strictest nun in the entire school and would not tolerate slowness. She opened the door of the office and sat down in the chair by the desk. Sister Diane surveyed her through thick glasses.

"Pupil 23, you have been here for one year this spring correct?" Sister asked rhetorically.

"Yes, Sister Diane," mumbled Nita.

"Speak up girl!" commanded Sister Diane.

"Yes, Sister Diane," said Nita a great deal louder than before.

"Well, after a year, we allow our pupils to go home for 5 weeks. You are going home for 5 weeks!" said Sister Diane.

Nita's heart fluttered and a smile found its way to her face for the first time since she had arrived at the school.

"Do you understand?" Sister asked slowly.

Nita nodded vigorously.

"There is a car waiting for you outside," the Sister told her.

The engine rumbled as the car started. Nita was too excited to sleep, but soon sheer boredom got hold of her and caused her to finally close her eyes. Nita opened her eyes and saw the familiar dirt road lined with the strong, thick pine trees that resembled fearless, proud warriors. Nita smiled. Images of warm embraces, bannock, and running through the field with her little brother, Anoki, danced in Nita's head. The car pulled into the driveway. Nita jumped out of the car and sprinted to the cabin. Nita pushed open the door of the cabin.

"Mama! Papa! I'm home," cried Nita.

"Nita? Nita!" her Papa cried, pulling her into a tight hug.

"Nita? My Nita?" screamed her mother as she ran full speed and grabbed Nita.

Nita hugged her parents tightly, breathing in their woodsy smell. Nita poked her head out of her parents' entangled arms.

"Is Anoki in bed?" asked Nita excitedly.

Her parents glanced at each other worriedly. Her mother's smile disappeared and a mask of sadness and fury replaced it.

"What?" Nita asked.

"We don't know where he is; we thought he would be placed with you." Sobbed her mother quietly.

"What? Why did you let them take him away? Anoki is gone forever because of you!" accused Nita, sobbing hysterically.

"Nita, Nita, dear sweet Nita there was nothing we could do. They told us we weren't teaching our children properly. They promised us they would take better care of you and Anoki than me and your mother ever could," sighed Papa.

"Our way of teaching was wrong," said her mother.

"What was wrong with our way?" asked Nita.

This time nobody had an answer.

LAND WARMED BY THE SUN
by Denise Marie Williams

My eyes were shut so tightly that I could see tiny shapes appear in blues and yellows on my eyelids. My hands clenched the top of my rolled-up wool blanket as I lay in bed waiting for sunrise. This would be my last day here at St. Mary's Mission and I couldn't understand how to feel. I had spent 10 years learning the white ways and I was thankful for my knowledge, but my heart ached and longed to be with my family.

There were other girls, older and younger than me who hated everything here. They hated what was taken from us and they felt injustice in the way we were treated. I watched their anger build through the years, and then die like a wounded animal will do when its heart is no longer in the fight.

I am always alone; I never join the other girls when they talk; I just watch. Now leaving, I can see that I know everyone, but no one knows me. I think maybe I will belong better with my family. Maybe they are watchers, too. I realize suddenly that they don't know me either.

Because I am sixteen now, I can't go to school at St. Mary's. I was only in school to learn white ways so I could become a good wife. That's what I understood from the others. I don't think I want to be a wife; I don't know what a "wife" is supposed to do back home.

I arrived at last to the place of my birth. My mother came toward me, and her eyes were wild with astonishment. I had seen this moment in my head for 10 years and as it happened, I watched it as though I wasn't there. She took my hands and shook them in hers; she was much older than I remembered. I walked to the house that I had memories of leaving as a child of six years old. I thought it would feel different; I thought I would be so happy, but the fear of what I didn't know or understand overtook me and I was scared.

I had three brothers who stayed with my mother. They were much older, in their 30s, and the biggest men I had ever seen. I didn't feel any connection to them, and I could see that they felt none to me. All three of them were there when I arrived; they said nothing and I followed along. I looked down at my shaking hands and shoved them quickly into my pockets. Did they hate me? Did they think I was white now?

That night dinner was being prepared, I watched my mother shuffle around the kitchen and over the tile floor that was thick with dirt. I wanted to clean it for her; in school nothing could ever be dirty like this. I stood up and took a broom from out of the corner in my hands. She looked at me in a blank sort of way, and as I put the broom to the floor, she took it from me with one sweep of her arm. Her hands pressed down on my shoulders as I was put back in my chair. What a strange reaction, why can't I help?

No one spoke English at home very often, most everyone in *Quw'utsun'* spoke Hul'qumi'num. Again, I was an outsider with almost no understanding of my native language. I thought and dreamed now in the white words. As the days went on in my new life, I realized that in school, I was an Indian amongst whites, and on the reserve, I was a white amongst Indians. I never felt bad for myself, but I did start to understand why the other girls were so angry that we had been taken. None of us asked to be different, but we were always being punished for it.

This new freedom took some getting used to. I waited for instruction, but when none came, I realized I was on my own. Eventually, I found what I think my spirit had always been looking for. All these years I knew I was connected to something and now, here it was. All at once, my senses came alive and my head swam with amazement and wonder.

The old trees reached high into the air; the branches were so thick I could not see the sky. Moss grew on everything and the ground was soft as I walked through it. The smell lifted my heart into my throat. I could hardly breathe, there was so much air. I touched everything as I found my way through the forest. I thought of my grandmother who had once told me that many years ago people fell from the sky and created us; they were our ancestors, and they lived only in the wilderness of this beautiful place. Today, I understood where I came from.

When the sun came down, I went back home. The doors of our house were left open and I could smell food as I approached. My mother stood in front of a small pile of nickels that were placed on the wooden table we ate. She looked at me, "Come here my beautiful baby," her hand out and her face encouraging. She piled some of the nickels into my hand, and we left for the Big House.

I could feel the drumming as we came close to this huge building in the middle of the reserve. I had a feeling that something was about to happen to me, but I didn't know what. As we entered through the heavy cedar doors, I was deafened by the Song that poured out of the people inside. I followed my mother closely and tried to copy her actions. We handed out money to the elders and to the families who had stayed here during the spring.

Around the fire they danced. There were masks and feathers; everyone was singing and chanting. Their voices went high and then low. I felt their spirits penetrate my heart; it was unstoppable as the smoke carried their voices through the holes in the roof. They pounded the ground with their feet as they switched directions and kept low to floor like warriors in a hunt. I wanted to join; I wanted to be a warrior, and my eyes were alive with passion.

Sitting in this huge building up high on the benches, with all of these Indians, made me feel safe. The 13 tribes that made up *Quw'utsun'* were all here supporting each other and showing respect. I didn't know that people could live like this. I was so proud, in this moment, that I was a part of this place where all was spiritual and respectful. This was not a white world.

As we left the Big House, I could smell the smoke in my hair and on my clothes. I was alive, and I was *Quw'utsun'*! We walked home with my mother's friend. The air was humid and night brought a damp chill away from the fire. I grasped my arms, one in the other as we walked. Running from behind, a girl caught up to us with the biggest smile I had ever seen. She had long brown hair that was matted at the top of her head. Her body was small and lean, but her feet were big, and her sandals flopped in the dirt as she ran. She looked at me as though she was happy to see me; I couldn't see why. Who was she?

Her mother introduced us, and she started telling me about her family and how they danced every week at the Big House. She grabbed my arm tightly and shook it; I could feel her fingernails stick into my skin. "Where's your jacket?" she insisted. I told her I had nothing to wear because I was at St. Mary's, and we wore uniforms there. I was surprised when she told me she had attended a residential school, too, but it had been closed by the government a few months back. She took off her jacket, a grey and white wool sweater with an eagle woven into the back. "It's yours now," she said grinning from ear to ear.

As I stepped carefully through the marsh of this wetland, I heard every sound that made this moment. My wool jacket gripped my body and rubbed my neck to make it itchy. I felt that this jacket was my right of passage. It was a token of my proud Indian heritage, which had come to be familiar to me little by little. The air was warm and heavy in my lungs, and the sun came down on my face cleansing my spirit.

Suddenly, geese flew up from the marsh. Straight into the air they went, darting together in every direction. They swooped back and forth, and I was captured in their noise. My arms shot up into the air; I held them there, feeling the spirit of the birds. I had felt this feeling before, so powerful and beautiful; they were like the people of *Quw'utsun'*. That day I could not speak to the birds, but they spoke to me.

I learned that summer about the people I was meant to be with all those years, and I was so proud. No one could ever take this away from me now. I felt that I was a whole person in my heart, nothing missing to wonder about. My mother told me that *Quw'utsun'*, in our language, means "land warmed by the sun," but I know this land is warm because of the people who live here.

MAKYA
by Trisha Redman

As Makya stood silently looking over the hill the little village, Para, below buzzed. Daily chores were being done. She could see women in the corn patches and men cutting and tanning yesterday's catches, a grandmother of the village sitting under a willow tree telling the smaller children stories around a fire while the older boys were practicing hunting and arching bows and arrows. The older girls helped their mothers with the babies, cooking and sewing.

Para lay beside the great waters with large rolling hills to its rear. The sandy beaches and open forest and fields were Makya's home. Makya's father was the leader of the warriors. Her mother had died giving birth to her. When her father had been at war, Makya stayed with her best friend Lily. Lily and Makya did everything together like sisters.

The older Makya got, the less she liked her father being chief warrior. When she was younger, she just didn't like him leaving her alone all the time, and now she always worried that he wouldn't come back. The more she watched the village, the more she saw its routine. Everything had its purpose and its reward. Nothing ever changed more than the leaves on the trees.

As she stood and watched, the winds picked up. On the edge of the beach there was a person coming her way. Slowly, she watched not one but two, three, maybe more men walking her way, with what looked like long wooden objects over their shoulders. Makya ran for the village. She called for her father at the edge of the houses. Everyone gathered around to hear why Makya was so panicked. When she started to explain, her father put his hand up for silence. She stopped talking and tried to calm her breathing.

Strange sounds were coming down the path. Almost like voices but in a language nobody could understand. It couldn't be another tribe because all the tribes around the village spoke the same. A far tribe wouldn't just walk into the village; there would be the drums of war first. Puzzled, everyone looked to the chief and the chief of the warriors. Many mothers took their children into their houses. At the path entrance appeared five men.

Their skin was the colour of the sand and their hair was the colour of corn. They pointed their sticks at the tribe and yelled. The closer they got, Makya realized it was not sticks they had. It wasn't anything she had seen before. They were gray, shiny, and hollow. Makya stood by her father and watched the men wander around their camp. Two of the men just stood with the gray sticks pointed at them, while the other three looked through the village. They never got close enough to touch anyone, but they kept talking to each other. Finally, they all grouped back together in front of the tribe. They yelled and waved their sticks and slowly walked backward to the path. Then they disappeared into the forest.

All at once, everyone started talking, asking the chief what to do, and what happened, and why the men came? The biggest question was who were these strange men and where did they come from? The chief ordered Makya's father and his warriors to get ready for battle. First, they had to see where the men went. Makya's father and two other warriors got bows and arrows and left to follow the pale men. Makya pleaded with her father not to go as he got ready. It'd be dangerous and could be a trap. He turned to her, hugged her, kissed her forehead and left. She followed to the entrance of the path pleading, but had to stand and watch him leave her.

Makya ran straight to Lily. Lily always made her feel better, but Lily was worried, too. Something wasn't right, so they went to see the wisest grandfather of the village. He didn't know anything about these strange men or the gray sticks. He told them to leave it to the warriors and the chief. That wasn't good enough. Makya and Lily made their own plan. If her father and the other men were not home by sundown tomorrow, they were going out to look for themselves.

At midday, Makya's father and the other men were back. They had followed the pale men back to a big boat not like the ones used by the tribe's fishermen. They were making what looked like a village on the sand beside it. But the warriors couldn't see in because of the large walls around it. There were two men at the outside doorway so no one could walk in like they did to the village here. The chief didn't like the sound of this; he wanted everyone ready for war. These men couldn't stay here.

The warriors rested this night because the next day, the drums of war would sound. This was a horrible night for Makya. She liked having her father home with her. She didn't want him to go to war and have to worry about him. She pleaded with him all night, for him to stay. Her argument was, "Let a younger man be chief warrior." He reassured her this was his last battle. He was getting too old for battle, but he couldn't run away now. This would be the biggest battle the tribe had ever had, and they would need him now. At sunrise, he was going to battle.

Watching the men suit up for battle, Makya's tears fell. As they put on their war paint and gathered their arrows, the tribe gathered to wish them luck and strength. The greatest grandmother of the village blessed them. The drums started to sound and the men walked. Lily and Makya stood side by side, hand in hand, watching the warriors leave.

Makya ran for the top of the hill. That was her thinking spot. Lily followed but didn't run to keep up. When Lily reached the cress, Makya was standing very still at the edge looking down. Lily silently walked over to see the last of the warriors disappearing into the forest. She put her arm around Makya and let her cry. Every battle her father had entered hurt Makya, but this one was very different. Something just wasn't right.

Makya and Lily went back down the hill after awhile. Chores still had to be done. Today was their day to be in the corn patches.

They picked up their baskets and headed out to the fields. There were no songs being sung in the fields today. Most of the women with the girls were warriors' wives. Everyone else was just listening, listening to the tears and the faint, dying drums of war. That night there was a meeting of the elders. Makya and Lily were to stay home with Lily's younger siblings. They were just putting them all to sleep when loud rings went off. Lily and Makya raced to the door to see what the strange noise was. There were five of the pale men standing in the middle of the village. Another one was standing with all the elders. The elders seemed unable to move. They had had their hands and feet tied together and to each other in a long line. One by one, one pale man pointed his stick at them, and that loud horrible noise went off again. When it did, that elder dropped. When Lily's father dropped, she ran out the door screaming and trying to get to him. Another pale man grabbed Lily.

Now Makya ran to help. She went around the first pale man, but the second grabbed her arm. He swung her around and she hit the ground. She could hear Lily screaming still, but she would only see the ground and a path to the elders. She felt his foot on her back. Makya twisted and kicked the man. Lily had bitten the man's arm holding her and freed herself. She ran to help Makya. Lily hit the man with the stick he had dropped trying to control Makya. They both ran to Lily's father's side. He was covered in blood. The elders were dead.

The pale men killed all the elders and men that night. All the young girls and boys were taken. Makya and Lily were among them. Their hands were tied together and their feet were all tied in a long line, so they could walk. One pale man walked in front, two behind him and the rest beside him. They walked to the beach.

As they went through the front doors, Makya could see that there was a battle last night there, too. Lily was the one to notice that the men lying face down were their warriors. She nudged Makya's arm and pointed to the right. Unmistakably, it was Makya's father. Makya screamed and pulled on the ropes to free herself. One of the men came beside her and hit her in the back of the legs with his stick to stop her.

They stopped near what seemed to be the centre of this little village. More pale men came out of their houses to see. There were lots of them but very few women. Screaming and yelling, the younger children were taken with force. Older children held on to them, trying to not let go but failed. The few women took them into a house and closed the door. The older boys were cut away from the girls and given shovels and hoes. The men started laughing and yelling at the girls. Two girls had their clothes cut off. They tried their hardest to cover themselves back up. The boys looked the other way not to offend the girls, but the pale men yelled louder. Some of the men walked up and down the line looking at the girls; one touched Makya's face. He put his hand on her head. He ran his fingers through her hair down beside her mouth. She bit him. He slapped her across her face, and Makya fell. Lily pulled on the rope attaching her to Makya. Makya looked at Lily, and they both had tears in their eyes.

Life changed that day. The boys from their village were the workers. They had to work the fields and hunt for the pale men. The pale women raised the younger children. They were being taught English and how to be "English." The girls had become slaves. They were to do whatever the pale men wanted. They had to cook for them, feed them and make their clothing. Most of the girls had been taken as wives to the men. They were to have the pale men's babies. Lily had gotten really sick. She was covered with small red bumps. She got weaker and weaker. Some of the pale men had this, too, and then got medication and help, but nobody gave it to Lily. Makya worked twice as hard so Lily didn't have to, and all night she put cool cloths on Lily's forehead. One night, Lily told Makya she thought she was pregnant. One of the pale men had violated her over and over again. The two friends talked all night and fell asleep in each other's arms. The next morning, Lily didn't wake up.

Makya knew what she had to do. With her head held high, she walked straight through the camp. She was going to find the man who hurt Lily. Outside his door she didn't hesitate. She picked up his gun and walked straight in. He was hurting another girl. Makya could see the tears in the girl's face. He yelled at Makya while he pulled up his pants. The girl covered herself and ran out the door. Makya wanted to hurt him like he hurt Lily. She lifted the gun at him. She had seen it used so many times she knew how to work one now. He stopped yelling and just stared at her. He laughed and tried to grab the gun. As he did, she flipped it around and hit him with the end of it. He fell to the floor. Her head was spinning. Just hurt him, she thought. He is the one who hurt Lily. She raised the gun again, but she couldn't do it. She just fired at the floor beside him. Two other English men ran in. They saw him lying on the ground with Makya standing there. They bound her and dragged her into the centre of the village. One yelled for everyone to watch. They shaved Makya's head to dishonour her and prove who she was. She was their example of what happens if people don't listen. From that day, until the day she died, Makya was just another slave for the English men.

THE POWER OF ONE AND ALL
by Kyle G. Wilson

WOLF WAS CAUTIOUS AND STEALTHY. Ever since law enforcement became present, everyone in Wolf's village had been subjected to injustice and inequality. Wolf himself was handled in ways that were very disrespectful and appalling. These strange people had tried telling Wolf's parents that they were practicing "satanic" rituals. If Wolf's family and everyone else were to continue these pagan traditions, they would go to Hell.

Tonight, however, Wolf's mission was to let his entire *House* know that there was to be a *Liseewa luuak*-- a death feast. The feast would be held at their local hall with those missionary camps only twenty or so metres away. This problem had been discussed and settled.

Ever since the Indian Act of 1876, the missionaries were scrounging within local communities across Canada to assimilate the "savages" into the "civilized" world of Europeans. The missionaries came to Kispiox, telling them that their life could be easier if they chose to enfranchise themselves. Part of the Indian Act's intention was to force the Natives across Canada to enfranchise if they wanted to be recognized as citizens in the country. Many of Wolf's relatives and neighbours chose to keep their status. Wolf did not understand; why did white men want his people to give up their traditions if they already had the Indian Act ripping apart their culture? Their death feast tonight was to recognize the head chief of the *House*. Without this feast, their *House* might fail to function because there would not be a new *House* chief to guide it.

To his left, he saw a flying owl peering down through the forest looking for its meal of the night. To his right flowed the stream that would serve as a quiet transporter of people and food to the landing site of the feast. His *House* was holding the feast right on the river bank; they had misled the missionaries to believe it was at the hall. This operation took swift action and became a community effort to divert the missionaries. As for the feast itself, it was to be held at midnight with all the high chiefs and wing chiefs, all the house members of Wolf's *House,* all of the elders in the village and most importantly, the person who had been selected to become the new *House* chief.

Up and down the Northwest Coast, many tribes had tried unsuccessfully to hold potlatches. Wolf's village, Kispiox, was not an exception. Many families had tried to hold feasts for their beloved dead or to give a significant name to a relative. These feasts dictated who had what powers, who had recognition of their status within the tribe and who was who in their society's hierarchy. Countless times, Wolf saw a neighbour dragged off in the night for alleged dancing, or drumming; countless times had he seen the police take away fathers, grandfathers, even children and women. All because they wanted to show their respect and acknowledgement of the dead, the memorable happy times, the heroic times and historic times in their family's history. It was a hard time for his people. They needed a leader, and they needed this feast.

Wolf took each step quietly, one step a tad quicker than the previous step. Soon he was sprinting through the forest with the alacrity of a wolf, making each step count, making each stride purposeful. It was only when he was sure that the missionaries' campsite was well out of vocal range, Wolf howled his practiced howl to indicate that all was right for the first canoe, with all the important chiefs, to make its way to the river bank and to ready themselves for a long night of dancing, chanting, storytelling and empowering speeches from the wise. He moved slowly back to the campsite, knowing his part of this scheme was in full swing; his part would decide whether this feast would be held at all.

Moonshine worked feverishly at her cooking spot at the riverbank. She had made enough food to last the whole night, enough to give out to the witnessing chiefs, to the one who would become chief, to all the guests from every *House* and just enough to hide for her brother Wolf. She was to see that the canoes came safely in and that everyone of importance was comfortable with his or her seating around the large circle. She was working on the Oolichans when she heard the powerful voice of Chief Gungootan singing the welcoming song.

Wolf had only one thing to say to the missionaries when they questioned him. "We are going to have a death feast at our hall come nine o'clock tonight." He did say that, and they believed him. *The only good thing about these white people is that they are very naïve,* he thought. He went with haste now to the very same spot in the woods to repeat his performance, only this time, he would be directing his howl to the campsite. *This should send off the guests*, he thought, *I must get ready for the hardest challenge in my life.*

Moonshine and the other women and men from the *House of Whitebear* were to help at this feast. Traditionally, the whole clan helped at the feast, but because there were so few guests, one *House* could single-handedly take care of all the business being done at this feast. The chiefs were settled now, and the only sound rippling the silent ambience, was another welcoming song. The guests were singing, coming down to the river. Moonshine was scared of what might be.

Wolf strolled towards his *House* through the woods. He had readied himself for what he would say to the white law enforcers. These white men had told him personally that "potlatches" were useless and had no value. They were unproductive and proved nothing. However, these white people had no understanding of how the Gitxsan enforced their laws and how their government worked. Wolf remembered his father selling drums, rattles, and special regalia, so that the white settlers would leave him and his family alone. If there were any items of importance to their culture, they would be destroyed immediately. Wolf's heirloom drum from his grandfather was destroyed that way. As Wolf went around from the backyard to the front yard, he saw a large white man in a uniform; he resembled authority. This officer had a rifle in his hand.

"Tell us where your potlatch is and we will let you off lightly. If you resist, you and everyone involved in this potlatch will suffer mighty big consequences."

"I might tell you where the death feast is held, but by then it might be over, for you are pretty late, *umshewa*."

Moonshine was wondering whether the fourth canoe would hold her brother. He had sacrificed everything to make this feast possible. It was her turn to be strong. She was a year younger than Wolf, and already she was a big part of a feast that would determine the future of her *House*. This was an honour not given lightly to anyone. She heard another song beginning. It was coming from the river. It was the last canoe, but her brother was not in it.

It was a long night of dancing, talking, giving, and discussing. The chiefs made a circle just outside the main circle to bring forward the new high chief of the *House*. It was morning when they named the successor of the high chief. Moonshine wept inside herself with sorrow. She knew Wolf did not have to do this. Other men wanted to be the bait. He chose his role; he chose to be the scapegoat to retain the life of his people. Moonshine felt embarrassed when one of the older guests saw her tear-streaked face. The older lady was Moonshine's auntie.

She came over to Moonshine and told her, "Your brother is a strong man. He will be remembered as the man who saved our people and our *House* tonight."

"What if the next generations don't live long enough to take what is rightly ours? What if those people ban our whole existence and call us animals who just happen to speak as they do? What if he is dead and they still find us when we feast?"

"Don't worry, Moonshine. He did what was right for our people. He chose to be a martyr for our cause. We sold many items to get the money for our feast. We traded many pelts to get our gifts. We asked every single man if he truly wanted to do this dangerous task. Your brother was the first one who said he would do it without fear."

Wolf was imprisoned and then taken to a strange building where people only spoke English. He was told that if he was to save his freedom, he must tell the truth or his family would suffer for his foolery. He looked through his narrowed eyes and saw an old white man in a black sinister cloak sitting upon a high seat looking down upon him.

Wolf walked along the path of sorrow. He knew that this ban of theirs did not intimidate his people. He had served his purpose to divert them from the Gitxsan's important decision about who will lead the *House* through disease and through these bad times. Ultimately, the new chief would see that Wolf had the proper warrior's memorial when he died and again, the death feast would occur right under the White Man's nose.

ELECTION DAY
by Cory Cappo

THERE ARE PEOPLE FIGHTING DOWN the road. Yesterday, I saw my older brother walk out of the house with a bat. He looked scared. All he told me was to "Stay put." I haven't seen him yet. My kokum's sitting on the couch watching TV

I ask her, "Kokum why is it like this?"

She tells me, "It's election time." Then she tells me to go to sleep.

I wake up to the sounds of men talking in the kitchen; I crawl out of bed and quietly sneak out of my room. I look out and see all the lights on in the hallway, kitchen and living room. I poke my head out and see my dad sitting with my uncles and my brother.

"Well I don't know about the Redfeather family, they don't seem like they're on our side this year!" my dad says as all his brothers laugh. My older brother, Steven, is sitting there with *a shiner*, smiling but not laughing.

"Yeah boy, you got 'em good," my dad leans over and puts his arm over my brother. He's been crying and is holding back tears. But he's still smiling. Seeing him like that makes me hold back tears.

"What are you doing up boy?" My mom, Linda, grabs my arm and sends me back to my room. I don't fall back to sleep; I push my ear to the door and listen.

"Well *bro*, we got 'em good," my Uncle Percy says.

"Yeah! I just said that!" says my dad.

"Well, we lost five votes there, that puts us roughly at about 235 or less depending how people react to this little… umm… little scrap," says Percy.

"We gotta maintain! Guys I want you to talk to your people and let them know this thing was not our fault. Okay?" My dad says with his tired voice.

"Yeah, we got it Tony. Don't worry," my other uncle, Sampson, speaks finally, after laughing for about five minutes.

They all get up and put on their shoes, except Steven. He sits there for about two minutes before he starts to whimper. My mother is already asleep. My dad is driving my uncles home. I take this chance to talk to my hurt brother.

I walk out the door for a second time. The lights are all on except the living room where Steven is lying on the couch. I sit across from him on a tiny chair.

"What's wrong?" I ask him.

"Nothing, go back to bed."

"No you're hurt. What's wrong?"

"None of your damn business. Now get lost before you get smoked."

"Fine then. Just thought I'd be nice. Not my fault you got hooked around." I say viciously. He gets up and walks right up to me and I'm cornered.

"I told you, you're gonna get smoked!" BOOM!

Damn, should've stayed in bed, I think to myself.

***

I wake up on the couch with my dad watching CNN. He sits on the loveseat opposite me. He stares and lights up another cigarette: DuMaurier King Size. He has been smoking them since I was born. People say they're bad for you. But I don't care that smell reminds me of him and home.

His name is Anthony Bear. He's thirty-six years old, and in his fourth year as chief of the Redtree Saulteaux First Nation, two and a half miles south of Saskatchewan's capital, Regina. He's not a big man as his last name implies, and he's not mean either. Well, as far as I've seen. I've been told he used to be a dangerous, angry young man in his younger days, but that's all I hear. These days he's quite mellow. Even with all the troubles surrounding him, he keeps a cool head. I try to be like him, but I can't. Being a kid with dietary problems can give one a lot of anger towards many people. But all in all, he's taught me well.

I wake up, sit up and he looks at me, smiling. Then it kicks in, the pain. My jaw looks like a purple grape. I got hit with a devastating right.

"Ow! Damn it, forgot all about that," I say.

"I thought I taught you how to avoid those shots, my boy." He throws me a bag of frozen peas, and I place it delicately on my chin. It soothes my pain, only temporarily. Until I remember I have school in one hour, and my bus will be here in ten minutes.

I am up and put on my clothes, and as sure as sun, my bus is here. I hop on the bus and sit next to my best friend, Benjamin Redfeather.

"What do you want?" he says with a sharp sting.

"Huh?" I say stupidly.

"I know what your damn family did to my dad last night!"

"What are you talking about? What did my brother do?"

"Your brother? So it was Steven?"

"Look bro, I don't know what you're talking 'bout."

I stopped and noticed the whole bus had stopped to witness me and my buddy's spat. I recuperated and struck back.

"Look, it's not my fault our dads are running against each other!" I thought I said, but I didn't. I meant to say it, but I didn't.

When I came to, I was sitting in the back seat of the bus being held down by my cousin, Mick. He kept telling me to calm down. The bus was moving now and I could hear everyone saying Ben's name and mine. Mick let me up and I saw everyone's eyes. They were viewing me carefully, the way a child watches for a bee. I looked down at my white shirt, which was now striped with red, and also my hands were looking as if I had been painting. I sat down and asked Mick what happened.

"Whoa! Bro, he started cutting up your dad and called you a fatty! Then you smoked him twice, and then he got you back with a few jabs that made your nose bleed."

"Well, did I win?" I asked out of breath.

"I dunno. I broke you two up before anything else bad happened."

As we pulled up to the school, I saw Ben walk out of the bus ahead of me with his nose covered up with a shirt. He walked into the school and sat with his cousins. All my cousins surrounded me, throwing shots, pretending a rumble was about to happen. A couple was telling each other how to throw a haymaker and others were singing "Bad Moon Rising" our "about-to-scrap anthem." I was still in a daze. Recovering from my trademark blackout moment, I read up on what happened to me. In a comic book *X-Men,* Wolverine has something called the "Berserker Rage." So I think I have that. It happens when I get mad. *Damn,* I think to myself, *I still got a whole day to go at school. How am I going to avoid the Redfeathers all day? That's it, just stick with the Bears, they won't try anything, yeah, that's it.*

First bell rings. The whole morning was a blur until lunch. Something always happens at lunch. I regroup with my cousins; we walk to the vacant laundromat and sit on the empty tables.

"Okay, I called this meeting to see what we're going to do about these bastards, the Redfeathers!" my oldest cousin, Rob, says. He and Steven were very close until Steven graduated and Rob stuck around. People said he was stupid. I just thought he stayed here to watch my back.

"Now, Freddy here just fought it out with Ben on the bus. Ben was cutting up my Uncle Tony and our family. We cannot let this slide; if the Redfeathers want a war, they'll get it! I've brought 100 water balloons!" A laugh erupts from everyone, even me. Of course, he was joking. He said that to calm us down. We all talk for a bit, and they ask me how I feel. Here I am, Freddy Bear, looking pitiful with a bruised jaw and a bloody shirt. Everyone thinks I got the bruise from Ben. I'm going to get him back; he's going to wish he never called me…BOOM!

I've just been hit; this day is going good. The Redfeathers snuck up on us, just like them to do something so sneaky. My ears ring. I run outside with all my cousins. The showdown is on... there are six of us against ten of them. I volunteer my pride and myself.

"Look! I'll just fight Ben. It's between us anyways!"

There were looks of acknowledgement coming from everyone. The fight was on. I walk towards him with my hands up and my chin close to my chest, my feet bounce and I get ready. Ben is also ready. We bounce at the same time; the unrest is building; the local storeowner turns on his sixties radio, and the sounds of old-school Credence Clearwater Revival blast through the streets. I smile and lunge forward. The fight lasts for as long as the Song does.

I heard it through the grapevine is stuck in my ears after and my knuckles and face are sore. I didn't go into my Berserker Rage. It was a good fight. So good Ben and I didn't notice the tears flowing down our faces leaving a clean spot through the blood and dirt. Rob picks me up and we walk to a back alley. He looks at me long and hard. With a cracked voice he asks, "You okay? Look, I'll get you home; you don't have to stick around this afternoon. I already got Little Jimmy to call your mom; she's coming here now."

The tiny car pulls up, soon after. My mom doesn't even look at me. I jump in and feel her shame towards me. She never liked the idea of me fighting. It is hot in the car and she doesn't even put on the air conditioning or even let me roll down the windows. That was the longest ride I ever took home.

When we pull in, I see there's a lot of traffic going towards the Band Office. I forget it is Election Day. We are going to see who will be the chief. My dad still, probably. We walk in the house and I see my kokum sitting there with a braid of sweetgrass and the sweet smell of smudge hits my nose and I instantly feel at ease. I sit next to her and brush the smoke across my face with my still bloody hands. I am about to go wash them when she tells me "Sit." So softly and sweetly, it commands obedience. I sit there waiting for the worst. It is quiet. I finally figure it out. She is waiting to hear what I have to say. I speak finally. Not knowing what to say, I blurt something out.

"Why is it like this during election time?"

She looked at me.

"You know, back before the white man showed up, we had our own way of doing things. Our people travelled with the buffalo and strong people governed our lives: spiritually and mentally. Some groups had leaders that passed on chiefs through bloodlines while others simply chose their strongest. It was a good system, no problems, people did what they had to do, and there was no trying to gain control over people with money or things with no value on the other side. What's valuable is in here…your heart and your soul; you have to be good to yourself and do what's right. I'm not going to give you heck about your fighting. I want you to ask yourself, was that a good thing for you to do? To hurt someone over small things that don't matter? That is what you have to think about. Will times ever change? That's not our place to know. For better or worse, things sort themselves out and in the end; all you get is how you conduct yourself and how you love other people."

She got up and left. I sat there thinking about what I'd done and wondered if Ben was okay. I hadn't noticed how tired I was. I lay down and instantly went to sleep. I slept for what felt like an eternity. I woke up to the smell of DuMaurier King Size cigarettes. I opened my eyes to see my dad sitting across from me, drinking coffee and looking at a sheet filled with numbers. I wipe my eyes, looked at the clock: 3 a.m. I had slept for twelve or more hours; my hands still have blood on them. My father looks at me.

"So? How did you do?" he asks.

"How did you do?" I ask right back.

We laugh.

"I guess as good as you," he says with a laugh.

I think to myself. We both did good, but both are sad of what we put our families and friends through in one day. We sit there, looking out onto the marsh in front of our house, glowing under the moonlight, both wondering what tomorrow will bring.

MY BROTHER LONNIE
by Chantelle Cheekinew

WHILE I WAS GOING TO the powwow with my brother, my kokum and moshum and four of my brother's friends, I got this feeling in my gut that something bad was going to happen. I didn't know why I was feeling this way so I ignored it. One of my brother's friends, Justin, had asked me if I was going to dance at the powwow.

I replied in a sarcastic way, "Nooo ..." and gave him a weird look.

He laughed and said, "Well are you?"

Then I laughed and replied, "Yes, of course!"

As I was entering the dance floor, just as I was going to dance, I could hear my brother in the distance calling my name.

So, I ran up to him and said, "What, what do you want?"

He replied, "Here, you stinker, here's that money I owe you," and gave me forty dollars to pay for a bet we'd made, and I won.

Lonnie was twenty years old and I was fifteen. Lonnie always babied me and was so over-protective of me, like all brothers are to their little sisters. Lonnie was the type of guy who knew everybody. He partied, but not a lot, though he didn't do drugs. He smoked, but that's it. Lonnie was always a ladies' man. I would always tease and ask him why he didn't have a girlfriend and his reply would be, "I'm taking my time. When I find the right girl out there for me, I'll let you know, so cut me some slack little sister," and he'd poke me in the belly.

Lonnie had always had disrespect for men who were women abusers because when he was growing up, he saw my mom get hit by my dad a lot. When I was born, my dad had left us and my mom died giving birth to me. Lonnie and my grandparents would often tell me stories about my mom. Sometimes they would end up crying while telling me a memory. I felt like it was my fault that she was gone because if she hadn't had me, she would still be here, but Lonnie always told me it wasn't my fault.

"Well, Lonnie, I'm going to go and dance now. OK, bye!" I tried to rush off but he yelled, "Hey, hey, hey, not so fast. Come here you little stinker!" I was thinking to myself when he said that, *Oh my god - there he is again babying me!*

I walked up to him and said, "What, what, what?"

He replied, "You're not going anywhere without me telling you this: go out there do your thing little sister ...make your ol' brother proud! WHOO!!"

"OH MY GOSH, LONNIE, STOPPIT - YOU'RE EMBARASSING ME!"

"Oops, sorry about that. I sort of got carried away! It's just I'm so proud of you! Ok, ok, I'll let you go and dance now! But I'm going to get something to eat. What do you want?"

"Hamburgers, french fries and a coke, please and thank you!" I said.

He smiled, "OK, go on now, you little monkey."

I laughed and walked off.

As I danced on the floor in my jingle dress, I listened to the drummers pour out all the love in their hearts and manipulate it into their singing. I waited for my moment when I would have to wave my fan in the air: that's when they would bang the drum three times. When I powwow danced, I feel so free, so happy and excited. I could feel my heart pounding along with the beating of the drums. I loved that feeling so much because it's better than any other feeling in the world! I had a passion for powwow dancing since I was a little girl.

I heard a gunshot in the distance where Lonnie was sitting with my grandparents and his friends and I thought to myself, *Oh no! Lonnie!!* I could hear women screaming and little children crying. I rushed to the area where the shot came from, leaving everyone else out there on the dance floor. When I reached the scene, I saw Lonnie lying on the ground. I ran towards my brother and tried to pick him up. Lonnie screamed in agony, telling me to leave him on the floor! I got his blood all over me. I cried, wiping away my tears of deep sadness and frustration. I screamed at everyone to call an ambulance but no one moved a muscle. When my kokum and moshum reach the scene, my moshum used his cell phone to call an ambulance. While we waited for it to arrive my moshum was telling Lonnie not to go to sleep, but like always, he didn't listen.

I held my brother in my arms. He coughed up blood and whispered, "Tessa I want you to do a favour for me ... be all you can be in life...don't make the same mistakes I made ... smarter people learn from other people's mistakes ... it's not that you're constantly making mistakes it's just that, I don't want you to end up like me... getting involved with gang shit and being involved with murders. Tessa, I know that you can do so much better than that, so don't do that kind of shit, OK? Make me proud lil' sis!"

He smiled and said, "Fuck, I'm so cold." Then I replied, "Lonnie it's so hot out I'm sweating."

He flashed me another smile and I cried, "Lonnie don't give up! Don't leave me! I need you here with me!!!" At that moment he died, just as the ambulance arrived.

I was holding Lonnie in my arms crying and swearing, yelling at his dead body "Lonnie, don't leave me," then one of the paramedics grabbed Lonnie from me and put his body on a stretcher. Just as they took Lonnie, I told them to be careful with his body.

Later that night, I was lying in bed crying, thinking of the accident and Lonnie's last words to me. Then out of nowhere, I saw my brother at the end of my bed. He stared at me with a cold look on his face. I was really startled.

Lonnie was talking to me, saying, "Don't be scared Tessa, it's only me!" he laughed. "Look, Tessa you can't be crying because I'm gone. I'm always by your side and watching over you! I'm in good hands now so you don't have to worry about me now, OK!" Then my shock went away and I wasn't afraid anymore.

I said to him, "I love you, Lonnie. I still need you here with me." Tears welled up in the corner of my eyes.

He replied, "I love you, too, and I miss you...and girl, I'm always with you. I'm watching over you! Well, Tessa, I have to go, that's him calling me, so see you around."

"Bye, Lonnie."

"No, Tessa, goodbye ain't forever...as cheesy as that sounds."

I chuckled and a lot of tears fell down my cheeks, and then he disappeared.

I woke up out of my sleep sweaty and confused, wondering if that was all just a dream or if it was real. I got up and looked outside. It was noon so I decided to go downstairs. Everything was quiet. My moshum went out hunting and my kokum was scrubbing my powwow outfit, trying to get out the bloodstain that Lonnie had made when I was holding him. I could see a lot of sorry and rage in my kokum's eyes. I could also tell by the way she was scrubbing and the frown on her face.

I said, "You know you don't have to do that," and she yelled, "WELL, IT ISN'T GOING TO COME OUT BY ITSELF. YOU WANT TO DO THIS?"

I replied as calmly as I could and without raising my voice, "Just because Lonnie is gone, you don't have to get angry and take your anger out on me."

She looked at me for half a minute then continued scrubbing. She broke down crying, "Oh, Tessa, I miss him so much. It's too quiet around here. I'm just so used to hearing him play his rap music loud, all the arguing you guys did over his music being too loud or dumb things, or even him being cheeky and gross by farting in your face while you were watching TV."

We both chuckled, and just remembering all these precious moments we had, made me cry because tears were running down my cheeks now. I rubbed away my kokum's tears and she rubbed away mine, like we always did when we cried together.

After that, I was telling my kokum to be strong like I was trying to be. I said to her, "Kokum, he's gone and he is in good hands now and someday we will all be reunited and I will finally get to meet my mom for the first time!" Excitement ran throughout my body, and I had a big smile on my face.

My kokum noticed and she said, "I bet you can't wait to meet her. She was a good woman but just met up with the wrong person. And you're right: Lonnie is gone and we have to face reality, we have to be strong and hold our heads up high. Things will be so different without him here with us, but I guess it was the Creator's choice to take him back home so we must move on with life." She sighed and gazed out the window.

I watched *Sweet 16* on *MTV*. While lying on the couch, I got this weird feeling like I was being watched and ohhh...I just knew it was Lonnie. It felt great knowing his spirit was still with us. I wanted to say something but thought I might look like a crazy person, so I just continued watching the show. Later on, my kokum asked me what I wanted to eat for lunch.

I joked and said, "Bannock and tea."

She chuckled, "How does bannock and duck soup sound??" and I replied quietly, "Mmmm, good!"

My moshum had gotten back from hunting and had caught a couple of rabbits. Just as he walked in, I ran up to him and gave him a big bear hug. He hugged me back, but the hug lasted long enough that I could feel his tears on my neck. I looked at my moshum and I said the same thing that I had told to my kokum, except he didn't give me heck.

My moshum went to sit on the couch and popped a smoke in his mouth. My kokum joined him and together they smoked and spoke in Cree. They thought I couldn't understand but I knew exactly what they where saying. My moshum was saying how it was too quiet in the house ever since Lonnie had passed on, and how he was used to going hunting with Lonnie and that it felt awkward for him to go alone this time. My kokum was agreeing, she also said that it wouldn't be too long until they were reunited with my mother and Lonnie. I got mad and went to my room and cried. My moshum and kokum came in my room and asked me what was wrong.

"You guys are going to be leaving me, and then who will I have left? Nobody! My mom is gone, my dad ran out on me when I was born, so I don't want NOTHING to do with him. I don't know anyone else; it's just not fair. Life ain't fair!" Tears ran down my cheeks. My kokum and moshum gave me a hug and told me that I'd be an older woman by the time they pass on, and I'd have my own little family by then.

Somehow, the things they always told me made me feel a whole lot better. They both were my medicine. They could make me feel better after feeling down and depressed and that was awesome. I loved my grandparents so much!

When I went to school on Monday, all I got was stares in the hallway. As people passed by me they would say, "Sorry to hear…" or "That's her, there she is…" I hated it so much. I hated when people felt sorry for me. I hated it when I felt sorry for myself. No matter how hard, I tried not to because kokum said it was the worst thing an Indian could do, and that was why most people committed suicide -- because they had felt a lot of self-pity. That wasn't me though; I always tell myself, no matter how hard times get I'd never take my own life because it's ridiculous and stupid. All it really was, was just a whole lot of self-pity.

I sat in English class not paying attention to the lesson the teacher was giving. I was pondering why all good things come to an end? Before Lonnie died, my life was all good. I was a powwow dancer - not anymore though. I had my boyfriend. I was not sure if we were still going out or not. I'd heard rumours that he was going to break up with me. I knew deep down in my heart that I just had to move on because like kokum said "Life goes on."

"Tessa, try paying attention to my lesson," shouted the teacher.

"Sorry, ma'am."

After school, I went home. My kokum and moshum asked how my day went, and I told them it didn't go too good, that all I got was stares in the halls. We got a knock at the door. It was my boyfriend, Daynen.

"Can I talk to you? Alone."

I replied, "Oh, yeah, let's go outside."

Then he said, "I'm sorry to hear about Lonnie – is everything OK?"

I replied "No!" and yelled at him, "Look, I know you came down here to break up with me, so cut the small talk and get down to business already!"

He said, "OK ... fine. It's over between us! We're done!" And he stomped down the steps. I turned around to walk away and almost forgot, "Wait, Daynen, I almost forgot! HERE!! You can have it back: I don't need it anymore!" I threw the necklace he had given me on Valentine's -- the first time he ever told me he loved me -- it was a necklace that said *I LOVE YOU* with a diamond in the *O* in love.

He replied, "All right, I see how it is Tessa. It's gonna be like that, then." He gave me this hurt look in his eyes and walked away.

My moshum drove us to the wake. It was held at the band office on our reserve. When we entered the front doors, all eyes were on me and I felt like screaming at the top of my lungs, "What are you looking at?" Instead, we just sat by the casket where my deceased brother lay. I had a good cry before the funeral. I looked at him and it just looked like he was sleeping. I remembered one time I snuck into his room when he was sound asleep, and I blew a blow horn and it was hilarious because he sat up straight and screamed like a girl saying he didn't do it! I laughed hysterically at him and he threw his pillow at me, and I ran off. All these moments I had with my brother I'll always cherish and treasure for the rest of my life. After the funeral, we just went home. Nobody really said anything to each other that day.

It is ten years later and I'm twenty-five. Two years ago, my kokum and moshum passed away beside each other, peacefully, in their sleep. I have three beautiful children and a handsome husband. Yup, I'm married...to my high school sweetheart, Daynen. We ended up getting back together the year my brother Lonnie died. That same year I stopped powwow dancing and still don't do it to this day. Now, I teach my daughters and my son to powwow dance. My son, Lonnie, dances *Grass* and my daughter, Metea, dances *Fancy* and my other daughter, Jocelyn, dances *Jingle*. I am finally at peace with myself. I might have lost all my family, my brother, my mother, and my grandparents but things are OK now. I guess it is true what my kokum said, "Life goes on." I have my own family to love and care about. By the way, I'm expecting my fourth child in June, the same birthday month as my brother, Lonnie.

MY LESSON
by Caitlyn Therrien

WHEN MY YOUNGER SISTER WAS named, we had planned a potlatch for many weeks. She was very honoured to receive the name which was once my grandmother's. All seemed to be exultant; there was food, gifts, song, and dance. I saw smiles on even the oldest of our elders. I didn't believe that anything could go wrong, but as my sister handed the blanket she was wearing to the chief, white men came between them yelling angrily. Apparently, one of the men was of great merit, and he told our chief that it was illegal for us to have such a gathering.

For many years we have had potlatches; it was a way for us to share wealth, to celebrate life, death, marriage, and names. Taking away our dances and our traditions was like erasing who we were from the face of the earth. We would not stand for anyone to take away what represented so much to us!

Although the whites had told us to stop, we would sometimes sneak to an area in the bush so we would not be caught, and in that area we would wear our masks, tell our stories, and celebrate the way of our people before the white man came.

My mother had once told me that the white man was trying to make us more like them, and I didn't understand why. I didn't understand why they wouldn't let us be when we had not done harm to them. I did not think that it was awful to be different from each other. Now at this age, I know that they were intolerant people, who seemed not to like anything that was different from them.

I remember when I was fourteen, white men told the parents in our community that they would benefit us more if we went to the white man's special schools. I remember my mother and father both weeping and watching them shrink smaller as we drove further away while my sister and I sat on a trailer with many other children.

At the school, I was given the name Catherine, I was not allowed to speak my own language and I was not allowed to have my own beliefs. I was taught to read, write and pray. If any of us misbehaved, we were beaten; we were not shown love, and we did not show love. To rebel we spoke our language out loud, calling many of the nuns bad names, and some tried to run away.

During one winter, several children had gotten a fever, and many of the ill children died; my sister was one of them. After my sister died, I was lost; I wished that I could have gone with her but instead, I stayed in that purgatory.

When I was finally sent home, I did not know who I was. I did not fit in with white people, nor did I fit in with my own people. My family did not know what to do with me, and I grew into a river of depression, anger and hate. For many years, I drank to try to console myself, but I found that could not help.

I could have continued this way to death. Until my mother, one day, took me to the forest where my sister was named and smudged me. She told me that I needed to find myself, to cleanse myself, and to save myself. I told her that I did not know how to do such things because I didn't know who I was. I told her of how I hated the white man for what they had made me become, which was a monster in my eyes. My mother took my hand and told me the story of our people. She told me not to hate the bottle but to hate the poison in it. She told me I was not lost because if I looked hard enough, I would realize that I was on the path that the creator had chosen for me, and to take each lesson I had endured and to use them to benefit my people. I now know who I am. I know my traditions; I am not ashamed of myself or of my people. I am very old now, and my life has taught me much, so as I give you this story, learn from it. Don't let any one take away who you are, and if you fall down, or forget, there will always be a reminder to help you pick yourself back up.

I teach you what I have been taught, so you can teach the same to your children. If we continue this, we have truly lost nothing, and we will never be forgotten.

OCCUPIED
by Joe Restoule General

THE WHEELS KEEP SPINNING AND spinning and spinning, stuck in a rut among the loose gravel. It's an uphill climb, as I push my daughter towards the bridge at the top of the path. I prefer the click-clack of the stroller on the uneven sidewalk stones over these two steps forward, three steps back monotonous dance. As I reach the bridge, I catch a glimpse of the flags crackling in the distance. The occupiers remain on the territory as my daughter sleeps a peaceful sleep.

It has been almost two weeks since the Ontario Provincial Police (O.P.P.) removed a handful of protestors from the Douglas Creek Estates building site. Another two months since the group took over the entrance to the site to protest the unresolved land claim. Another eleven years or so since the federal government was made aware of the issues surrounding these lands originally given to the Six Nations of the Grand River in the Haldimand Proclamation. Just over a year since the night my daughter entered this world.

I'm not sure if it's curiosity, thirst, or absolution which brings me near the simmering stand-off between the O.P.P. and the Native protestors, as the media refers to them. Right now, the only thing simmering is the heat, as officers sit in squad cars at every entry point to the Estates, probably doing their public duty to remain in the shade. Meanwhile, protestors make the journey to cool libation half a mile up the road at the local Tim Horton's, passing through the barricade and the squad cars without notice.

I've seen these images on TV. It's the third squad car that surprises me, parked at the end of a dead-end street. As I wheel my daughter in her stroller away from the dead end, we cross the road to get to the other side. Though I haven't been in this neighbourhood in awhile, I'm taken aback by the outpouring of patriotism more commonplace in an American suburb. Every third house sports a brand new Canadian flag, not yet faded by the afternoon sun. They hang limp, not yet accustomed to the wind's caress, and denied free movement by the starch hangover of plastic packaging.

I peek inside the sunroof of the canvas canopy to be sure my daughter hasn't stirred. She lies with her hands and arms above her head as I pass a fourth squad car at yet another dead end. I'm walking in circles.

An elderly couple blocks the sidewalk ahead of me, so I slow my pace down so as not to scare them. They're dressed in salmon sweaters and khaki pants, carrying bags of groceries from the nearby supermarket. It's difficult to navigate around them, as their walk is slightly crooked, and the woman is at least seven feet ahead of the man. I take to the grass, trampling the dandelions, and the man takes notice of me.

"Excuse me," he says in a hoarse growl.

"Oh, I'm sorry," the woman says upon hearing her husband's voice.

"No problem," I reply, and continue past the Catholic school. There's a sign outside celebrating Catholic School Week. Oddly self-congratulatory. This school was shut down the day of the O.P.P. raid. Public safety was a concern. Apparently someone in power thought the Natives posed a threat to the children inside. Or perhaps it was the O.P.P.'s own actions which may have been contrary to the public well-being. It's never been explicitly stated.

Kitty corner to the school, I hear children screaming and squealing. I see two young girls skipping through the sprinkler, cooling off on the nicest spring day of the year. Possibly they are celebrating Catholic School Week from home. I imagine my daughter hopping through the hose spray when she comes home from school.

"What did you do at school today, sweetheart?"

"We had a social in the morning and watched *Finding Nemo 2*," she replies.

I'm distracted by a milk carton twirling from a tree branch. A homemade bird feeder welcomes the soft, warm breeze, and I look for my daughter's fingerprints on it. What will hers look like five years from now? Her future feeder?

My thoughts are interrupted by the sound of a backhoe arguing with a bulldozer. Construction sounds fill the air, drowning out the girls' screaming and causing my daughter to rustle in her stroller. You can put a stop to one construction site and two others take its place. I pick up my pace, speeding over chalk outlines of preschoolers etched on the pavement in sidewalk chalk. Each has a name scribbled beside it, in memory or recognition. It hasn't rained in sometime, and I can't imagine when these ghosts will be washed away.

Even though my daughter is sleeping, she brings smiles to people's faces. At my brisk pace, home owners between dwellings with flags smile, nod their heads, and say a friendly greeting. This small town spirit feels odd in context of the current occupation. I can't tell if the residents' greetings are on account of my very beautiful young child, which all parents can relate to, or whether they are going out of their way to express their kindness, as if to say, "We're on your side. Don't paint all of us in Caledonia with the same brush." Perhaps that's why I'm taking my daughter into town on a peace walk. To say the same thing about First Nations.

It's hard to ignore the fact that this sleeping wonder, this harmless child was once the image of the warriors who stand behind the barricade, wearing a bandana to conceal that peaceful face. That one day, this snoozing child who elicits smiles from non-Native residents may one day be the one awakening her people to the unresolved land claims. A future leader asleep in the present, dreaming of an outcome to this historic occupation which eludes us for the time being. Will this issue be history by the time she comes of age, taught in school as the day the Canadian government agreed to negotiate with the Confederacy council, for the first time in over 80 years, when in 1924 they forcibly removed the hereditary government by gunpoint? Or will she be forced to see history repeat itself, over and over again?

I pause at the top of the hill, in the middle of the bridge which carries us over a small creek. I look to the sun and follow the flow of the creek as it splits the park in two equal sections. On one side, there are a thousand dandelions, a massive army of yellow and gold taking over the hillside. On the other lies a solitary, strong tree. An evergreen, alone among the grass, not a dandelion in sight. The smell of freshly cut grass fills my head.

I cross that bridge and ponder the historic nine span bridges that cross the Grand River in Caledonia. With the blockade, increased traffic has been diverted over the concrete structure built a couple of years after the Indian Act. There's always been concern about the long term strength and stability of the bridge and this stand off continues to apply pressure to the bridge. I can't help but feel the weight crushing the pillars of the past and whether or not this added pressure will perpetuate the bridge's inevitable collapse.

Just then, my daughter wakes up, springing to life, as a Yellow Warbler flies past her field of vision. She giggles with delight, seeing something so beautiful, so peaceful, and so gracious for the first time. I want to join in her laughter.

STEH-WAH
by Kerissa M. Dickie

ANNIE TUCKED A STRAND OF bluebells behind Margaret's ear, and rubbed out a streak of dirt from her small cheek.

"*Etánana...* you look like your big sister, Gloria."

Margaret smiled back at her, her chubby cheeks turning her eyes into crescent moons. The summer sun settled into her braids, sand peppered in the part and glittered. While she admired her daughter, a blanket of darkness fell over the riverbank. Annie looked up into the sky and sighed—a pack of grey clouds had begun to stalk the sun. She lifted the pail of river water to her hip and climbed the bank, stopping every now and then to dig her fingers into the soil to regain her balance. Margaret followed in her tracks, half-crawling on her knees, growling like a bear. Erwin, only a few months old, was jostled awake by the awkward climb; he was wrapped tightly onto Annie's back, in a blanket that bound Annie's chest into a flat and aching mound of sweat and milk.

Their camp sat on a smooth plateau above the Liard River, which snaked through infinite forests of pine, poplar, and marshland. A tent of stripped young trees covered in old canvas sat back near the tree line; a food box stood high above the ground on the opposite side of the clearing, and between the two was a fire pit dug deep into the dirt with a blackened frying pan and kettle sitting in the cold ashes. Annie brushed off dirt and pebbles that had stuck into Margaret's shins.

"Help *Mó* find some kindling for the fire. When Gloria comes back from checking the snares, she might have *Gá* for us to cook!"

They walked back into the brush, Annie dancing with her shoulders and hips to help calm the baby on her back. Erwin's arms were wrapped tight enough to her body that he couldn't fuss or scratch at his face as he was most likely to do otherwise. His whimpers and grunts quieted once they entered the canopy of the forest, Annie's and Margaret's feet making the mossy ground crunch and whisper beneath them.

"*Mó*! Big stick!" Margaret pointed up at a long branch, high on a pine, with twigs like splayed, broken fingers.

"*Elé, Babeha*.... that one is still alive. The live ones have water inside, and they won't burn good. The dead ones make the best fire." She hunched over, and pressed a rotten twig into Margaret's hand.

"Look for sticks like this."

"*Heh Mó*," Margaret set out like an animal on the prowl, yelling excitedly with every twig she collected into her arms.

Annie smiled back at her, rocking from side to side to soothe Erwin. By next year he will be walking; Annie's first instinct being to chase after him and clutch him to her chest. Gloria will be taken shortly after she turns eight. Margaret and Erwin will be taken even younger. Because of residential school, none of her children will ever really know her.

* * *

Henry McLeod was friends with her father. He would come by the house and drink tea with her parents. The first time they met, Annie was twelve years old and had just finished making some bannock. Henry cut a large hunk off, covered it in a thick layer of lard, and ate it all in three bites. With melted lard spread across his chin, he grinned up at her and she shuddered inwardly. He was very handsome, and had a good job—working for the Hudson's Bay Company—but something about the way he looked at her made the bannock she had just swallowed, feel like it was backtracking into her mouth. He was younger than her father, but already had a dead wife and a little girl.

A few months later, Annie's parents were on the trapline, and she was enjoying being old enough to stay behind and take care of her brothers. They were busy playing in the trees back in the bush, and she had just finished filling a small tin bowl with raspberries from the bushes crawling along the brush of the tree line. She was holding the berries in her hands, dipping a cup into the water barrel beside the front door and spilling it over them and onto the dry dandelions below. Bugs the colour of leaves, crawled up her thumb and onto her wrist. One of her little brothers let out a strangled cry from somewhere in the bushes, and muffled little voices giggled in reply, and bodies crashed back through the brush.

Henry appeared from the side of the house, and smiled at her. "*Nedago Nezu,* Annie?" He was dressed in a dark button-down shirt and tweed trousers; his hair was slicked back with grease, and he carried a pack over his shoulder. He had skin the colour of *denètū*, a rich dark reddish-brown root, and straight, clean teeth. His eyes crinkled at the corners, dark lashes almost touching his cheeks when he smiled.

"Are your parent's home?" He stood in the doorway, one foot inside. He watched Annie fidget with a seam in her skirt, while she tried to think quickly. She felt her knees start to shake.

"No. They're on the trapline." She picked a small stem out of the tin of berries and flicked it onto the floor.

Henry walked into the kitchen and stood beside her. "That's too bad." He looked into her eyes, picked a berry from the tin, put it between his lips and used his tongue to pull it inside his mouth. Annie felt a strange sick feeling tighten around her skull; it stiffened her back, dug into her throat and made her want to scream. Then he was on top of her on the dirt floor, the smell and taste of spruce gum in her mouth, and dirt in her eyelashes. Afterwards, he kissed her hair, pulled her skirt back down over her knees and left her lying in a heap on the floor.

When night fell, her brothers were asleep as soon as they lay down on the spruce boughs, but she lay silent, clutching an old rag doll to her neck. She cried soundlessly into the flowing fire-coloured hair she once imagined it to have.

* * *

    Annie sits on the floor inside her closet, with her legs tucked beneath her. She pulls photos from boxes in handfuls, shuffling through them and dropping them into shiny masses on the floor. The rims of her eyes are a vibrant red, tears streak down her cheeks, and run from her nose. They're all pictures of her life with Henry: sixty years, eleven children, separate bedrooms. Annie holds onto the door frame for support, gets up with a sharp breath, and turns to look down at the piles of snapshots by her feet. She pushes at them with the toe of her slipper, sends those closest to her scuttling into the back of the closet.

    She remembers being twelve years old, standing on a riverbank and smiling for a picture being taken by an Indian Affairs agent, this being before agents took children. She had just climbed out of her father's boat, and her feet were bare. The sand was cool, and a white man with a kind smile gave her a hard rock of candy. She sucked it until it disappeared on her tongue. Seeing that picture would always remind her of that sweet, buttery taste in her mouth and of the river water passing quickly beneath the boat, and the way her fingertips could leave trails on the surface. She was just a *steh-wah*, a little girl.

    Now, Henry was dead, and the picture was nowhere to be found. If only she could find it, hold it in her hands... then she could remember.

    The bed creaks as she lies down; she pulls the quilt up to her nose and stares up at the ceiling. It's been one day since Henry left this world, and all the sleep she has gotten since has brought only nightmares: owls trapped in rabbit snares; rivers with no water; bear tracks circling her tent. Annie can hear the muffled voices of her children creeping in under the door, talking about Henry. Community leader, businessman... and he started it all from nothing. When someone found out he was orphaned as a baby and raised in a residential school on top of it all, their eyes almost crossed in astonishment.

* * *

Henry and Annie were married by a transient priest soon after Annie turned thirteen years old. Henry was 25, and his young daughter, Gloria, had been without a mother for almost a year. His first wife, Marie, was taken by T.B. the winter before. Annie was much younger than he, but she would be a good mother, and could already scrape and smoke moose hide by herself. They would be a good match, and her parents were accepting of the arrangement.

When he first took her down river to his camp, she ran away—wearing just her moccasins and a threadbare dress, and he arrived at her parents' camp the next morning and found her clutched onto her mother's skirt and howling. Her father, Joseph, hit her with willow switches and forced her back into Henry's boat.

Henry started moving his camp further and further down the river, with Annie running away each time he let her out of his sight. Once the weather got cold at night, and Annie's belly grew too big with pregnancy, she finally gave in and could be trusted to walk along the riverbank by herself.

More than just feeding and caring for Gloria, Henry's little girl, she and Annie became friends. They would sit in the soft silt of the riverbed and make dolls out of scrap pieces of fabric—Annie teaching the young girl how to thread the needle. They would set rabbit snares before nightfall, and wait eagerly for the morning.

That spring, under threats by an Indian Agent to take their children unless they moved closer to a town three days south by boat, they abandoned their camp and began their journey. They had three children with them, including Gloria—who pretended the new baby boy, Erwin, was her own. With every stroke in the river, Annie felt her heart grow farther and farther away from her mother, but crying wouldn't change the current.

* * *

That afternoon, the Catholic Church was filled with people. A priest with a strong French-Canadian accent spoke at the podium, and read aloud from a shiny new bible. After he gave the usual service, Erwin got up and headed to the front. He stood only a few feet away from the closed casket. It looked like a giant cake, the lid covered in a fragrant layer of white and yellow flowers. Erwin reached for a large piece of poster board plastered with old photos that was balanced against the casket.

"My father lived a long, rich life, and I know he left without any regrets. He was a good man and a good provider, and he loved his family." He motioned to the pictures taken of Henry and his family as he talked.

The picture of Annie standing beside the riverboat was tacked onto the bottom of the page. Erwin's words started to swell and echo inside her head, and suddenly Annie gripped onto the pew with her fingernails. A huge emotion she didn't recognize began to rack through her body, constricting her muscles. She squeaked. Annie squirmed out of her seat, and stood up. A crowd of suits and bolo ties and teary faces looked up at her in surprise. She smoothed out the torso of her dress, stepped over feet and made her way into the aisle, almost tripping on her daughter's purse.

"Mom, are you okay?" It was Carole, Erwin, her next door neighbour, the guy who owned the grocery store; it was everyone watching her, waiting. She strode quickly to the front of the church, grabbed hold of the poster board and ripped her picture off the page. She turned, and walked briskly down the aisle, almost at a jog, pushed through the doors and collapsed to her knees onto the sidewalk in a bundle of jagged nerves.

A roar of wild laughter ripped from Annie's throat and into her palms, both shocking and relieving her. She held the photo of herself as a little girl to her chest and laughed until her stomach muscles ached, until tears ran from her eyes, until all of her energy drained and left her light-headed. The clear sky above her was ecstasy, rapture.

It was this way that Anabel and Erwin came upon their mother, and realized how small their grief must have been in comparison.

GOING THE DISTANCE
by Sara General

"Are you certain?" his voice shook. Decker nodded, and his face broke into a smile. Deskaheh turned from him and looked out across the city, where the moon reflected off the windows of quiet houses. Warmth was rising into his face, and his cheeks flushed with the success of knowing that after all of these days he had been here in Geneva, that it at last might come to something. A nation, he knew, was more than a word to be used in meetings. It had to be carried by its people, in their hearts and minds, and so much of their hope lay with him.

***

"Good morning! Happy birthday sweetie." She smiled wearily and sat down at the table. A birthday card had already been set down next to her place, and she poured some coffee into her cup, eyeing it with interest.

"One year older, it's all downhill from here." Her father cautioned her, his eyes still absorbed in a pile of papers.

"Yeah, I suspect it is…this is a little thick…money?" She asked, grasping the card and rubbing her fingers across it.

"Oh, yeah right." Her mother joked, appearing with a steaming pan of eggs and throwing some down on her plate. She shrugged and opened the card. She knew it wasn't money, but this had been their little joke over the years anyway. Her parents had made a bit of a tradition out of collecting interesting little facts about the day their children had been born and setting them in their birthday cards. One year, her sister's birthday had fallen on the same day that Nelson Mandela had been freed. She suspected that they might be saving that one until Anya was a little bit older to appreciate it. She scanned the card, and thanked them, then proceeded to open the paper that had accompanied it.

September 4, 1923
Chief Deskaheh of the Six Nations presents 'The Redman's Appeal' to the president of the assembly of the League of Nations, in Geneva, Switzerland

She bit into her eggs and considered the paper. "What's this?" she asked. "I've never heard of this."

Her father shrugged as her mother set some toast down next to her. "I don't know. I wanted to put that it was the season finale of Gilligan's Island, but I picked last year."

"Oh yeah, that painting that was auctioned off in 1875 or something after being missing for a hundred years."

"And who was the painting of?"

"Georgiana Spencer-an ancestor of Princess Diana," (Her mother beamed at the name). "It was stolen by Adam Worth, which was cool because he was the inspiration for Dr. Moriarty!"

"Who's that?" her mom asked.

"Sherlock Holmes' eternal enemy, of course! Anyways, I've never heard of this guy." She said, looking to her dad for an explanation.

Her dad smiled as he looked, flipped his page. "Well, now you do. Go sleuth it out."

***

The room had grown almost bitterly cold and still the Minister had not so much as poked at the fire. His desk was piled heavily with letters, maps and reports. He flipped through them quickly and not at all gently.

"They called the King their lord, they used those words-it's all in the language they use. You can do this, Duncan, it's all in their words and how you present it. If you present it in just the right way, it will work..." he muttered. Endlessly he repeated those words. The door creaked open, and he glanced up startled.

"Good evenin,' Minister. Just came in to tidy but if you're not done, I'll just check on your fire and be on my way. Won't be disturbing you." The evening staff had already arrived, which must mean it was hours since everyone else had gone home.

"Not at all, Mr. Evans." He replied curtly, and turned back to his work.

Evans added several pieces of wood and poked at the coals. "Working late this evening, Minister?"

"That's right." He glanced at the clock and sighing, he turned to the window.

"And every night," he murmured, "until this situation has been brought to hand. It won't do. It just won't do to let him remain there. He has to be brought down, but how?" He rubbed his forehead, contemplating his options.

"I just wanted to say sir, my wife and I, we read your recent poem. And she was touched, sir, by your experiences with the Indians. You really do them an honour Mr. Scott."

"Mmm...quite."

***

Louise entered the house and pulling some papers out of her bag, she flung it to the floor.

"Just thought you'd give me a nice cheerful birthday, huh?" She accused, throwing the papers down on her dad's desk.

"Nonsense. I thought you'd be pleased with the connection." He looked up, surprised.

"Pleased! Pleased? How could I be? The whole thing came to nothing didn't it? Deskaheh stayed there for a year and for what? To be told that the affairs of his nation were a domestic concern of Canada. You know he died shortly after."

"Louise, please-"

"And not only did he die, in the United States; nonetheless, he couldn't even come back, but the whole time he was there, this Duncan Campbell Scott man, was working to discredit everything he was doing."

"Yes, but-"

"This man was the Minister of Indian Affairs for like 50 years! How is that possible that someone so cruel could stay in office that long! He was terrible; he concocted the residential school system with that Ryerson guy. He even wrote poetry! Ha! Have you read his poems?" She stopped to take a breath.

"Yes, they're…"

"Propaganda's what they are!" She cut in, her oxygen restored. "And I won't even get started on the elected council." She stopped abruptly and glanced at the floor, fully aware that the frustration her research had created was not in any way directed at her father.

Sensing her guilt, he smiled at her and gestured for her to sit down. "Ahh, it's good to get a little angry once in awhile. But it can't last. Nothing can be done well that's done in a temper. But you're right, at least partially. We came to this territory in 1785, after the Confederacy had a difference of opinion over which side to take in the war: American or British. We surrendered some land to make money to sustain us. Some people say that never happened, they just can't see it. In some cases they were right; it was fraudulent. But I can imagine that the hunting wasn't all that good and we had to do something to feed our families. Our lifestyle was changing. Decisions were made Louise; actions were taken. We were influenced by the Europeans in some ways and in others we weren't. This all happened even before Deskaheh went to the League of Nations to insist that we were in trouble, and that we needed our own ways to see us through it," he said this all very calmly.

Louise stared at the ground. "I get that history is biased. I get that there has to be some kind of agreement over what really happened and how to deal with it now, but I don't get why I haven't heard about this before? Any of this."

"Because they don't teach this in schools, Louise. And they should. A lot of foolish things happen amongst people when they don't understand all the facts. Imagine if everyone felt differently about what to do at a stop-light? I'm sure some of your friends don't understand what makes you First Nation."

She nodded. "And I haven't known enough of this history to explain to them."

"Right, but it isn't your responsibility entirely. You have one, don't get me wrong. But if you want a nation of people who are understanding and not racist or discriminating, then you have to provide them with the tools to live that way. Which I hardly need to point out to you, means sharing a lot more history than you are getting now."

She nodded again. He smiled at her. "I didn't choose this piece to ruin your birthday. I, myself, think it was pretty remarkable to go all the way to the League of Nations in 1923. The first bit of international activism for our people. I always like to think that we were the first league of nations, you know. Six independent nations coming together after being at war with one another for so long. We formed the Great Good together, and I think there is something to that. Or should I have let your mother pick the Gilligan's Island thing?"

She smiled. "No, this was fine. Now where's my real present?"

***

I learned that day that it takes a great deal of strength to admit that your people are weak without giving up altogether. I have seen firsthand, the effects of years of oppression on my people. It has not only made them victims, but aggressors as well. Which I suppose follows some sort of pattern of violence.

A few months after that birthday, a situation emerged from a land claims dispute on my reserve, and we were thrown back into the past to contemplate over 200 years of history. We have become divided in our understanding of the past. Some of our people aren't always able to grasp the Great Good. And their anger has brought out centuries of accumulated hurt, and a great deal of that anger has been misdirected and downright pointless. It has had effects on our non-Native neighbours as well, and not all of it good or bad. But it made me writhe to know that for years this information had been available, and that no one had made use of it. How much easier would it be to solve our issues if everyone was educated in them? Because we aren't just arguing about history with the government, we are arguing with ourselves. It reminds me of Question Period.

It has been especially hard watching everyone scramble for information, for the ever- dangerous word, the ever- confirming document that will settle what we are forever trying to build -- a future where our children speak our language, the people fill the Longhouses on all the ceremonies, not just the big ones, and no one questions their identity as Haudenosaunee. Because they know they belong and they can feel it. It will be hard because we have adopted many practices that aren't our own, that come from a different way of reasoning than our own, and I am not sure if we are willing to give them all up.

We have hung in that balance for a long time, and Deskaheh knew it. And standing here by the Grand River, wondering what it must have looked like to him-- a thousand times cleaner, no doubt-- I wonder if he could have the hope now that he had then. We still had our languages when he was here; we still had a chance in that way. But our only chance now, is to accept what is done, to decide what we want for the future, what we can save and how to achieve it together.

They say that Deskaheh died of a broken heart, the dream of freedom and sovereignty still glistening in his eyes. But dreams do not die with us, and the power of a nation does not disappear because a leader passes. It doesn't disappear because the boundary lines change. It is an ever changing thing that is carried by the hearts and minds of its people. By men and women with peace and a good mind that use words to communicate not sting, who create ideas not conflicts, who choose life over survival. As long as there is even one chance to have this kind of dream, I think I can believe in it because it is one that I don't have to achieve on my own, even if those who had it first have long been gone.

ACROSS THE BARRICADE
by Alicia Elliott

IF YOU'RE A MIDDLE-CLASS Caucasian male like me, your life is measured in how many victims you make of different minority groups. You can never be the victim; political correctness forbids it.

Following this line of thinking, the so-called "racist card" is only available in non-white community decks. Obviously, it's a trump no matter what is played before it. This gives me little faith in Canada.

My city is being held hostage by Indians. Any attempt to protest this, is being stamped as "racist" by every minority-loving media outlet in the country. My government has done nothing to stop the Indians from blocking our roads. The police have not acted on a court injunction to remove the protesters from the land they are occupying. Since the moment Caledonia residents started voicing our objections, we've had to wear the ugly label of "racist."

After seeing this and experiencing this, Canada isn't the country I thought it was at all. It's merely the country equivalent of a gawky boy too afraid to stand up to the school bully.

The same people I see right now across the police lines and tarp-laden barricades, not three months ago were living in harmony with the town of Caledonia. No one would ever have thought something was wrong. We had no idea what level of hatred lay behind their stoic courtesy.

I've heard some folk say that the Indians have been planning this for a year, stockpiling tires to burn, intricately organizing every detail of my hometown's strangulation. Nearly every detail, anyway.

The part that they overlooked was the history of the lands they say are theirs. Everyone in Caledonia knows by now that the Natives sold their land to Canada in 1841. Conveniently for them, however, time is on their side.

The Ipperwash inquiry is still looming over Canada, making the government too afraid to assert anything against any Native, criminal or not.

"Leave it to him to want to trample more rights," an older man to my left says. "He's king of the *turds*."

A few chuckle at this, but the two silhouettes the man is referring to just beyond the police cars, act as attention magnets.

Though the curtain of twilight is falling quickly, I can tell that one of the figures is one of them. The other, uniformed in dark blue, is obviously an Ontario Provincial Police (O.P.P.) officer.

It's nearly 8 p.m. Now, and for another night, I've drifted to the roadblocks to meet with other residents as frustrated as I am. There are few people now, but once the sun kisses our town good-bye for the day, more will join our ranks.

"What's going on?" I ask the old man.

"That damn Indian wants the O.P.P. to move the police line back. They want to cut off Canadian Tire's parking lot because they're scared. They think we're the violent ones," he rasps, raising his voice for everyone to hear towards the end.

Those Indians across the barricade are the ones that moved onto a land site and stopped construction, nearly bankrupting the developers. They blocked off our south road, effectively slaughtering many people's way to work and emergency vehicles. They are the reason my parent's property value dropped $30,000. We couldn't give our house to a homeless man at this point. They, with their drums and dark complexions, are the monsters in my little brother's nightmares and the surreal tormentors just a chain-link fence away from his playground. They are breaking the law, but yelling "racism" should the police try to enforce anything. Canada won't touch them. The O.P.P. won't touch them. Yet, somehow, we are scaring them.

"Good. Maybe we should drive 'em off since no one else has the spine to," I yell, to much applause. Things will never be the same.

I've seen their angry eyes on the television and read their spiteful words in the newspaper. Though I haven't actually been to one of Caledonia's displays of aggression and prejudice parading as a protester, I feel like they are glaring at me, screaming at me through the flat images. Fear is not a strong enough word to describe this horrible isolation.

****

Up until that first rally, my long ebony hair and dark skin were emblems of pride, wordlessly announcing to all, my Mohawk heritage. Now I wish I could disappear from or mask other's glances, choose who finds that out about me.

It is resonating in my ears still, though they stopped chanting twenty minutes ago.

"We want blood! We want blood!"

The 11 o'clock news would never air footage of that. The Canadian media much prefer to spin our voices and our much less violent wants.

We want understanding, justice. We want to celebrate our ancestry without a foreign government trying to squeeze us into the "good, non-ethnic citizen" mold at every turn.

Peering over my father's shoulder, I see the indistinct shadows of Caledonia residents. From this distance, they look like a black, shapeless cloud, occasionally illuminated by the police cars' lights.

I wish I could cross the barriers just once and talk to the Caledonians without them turning off their ears and closing their minds upon seeing the colour of my skin. Maybe if I could explain to them what really happened in 1841, they would stop harassing us and get angry with the real criminal here: Canada.

As soon as we were given six miles on either side of the Grand River by the British Crown, the Canadian government wasted no time using slippery wording and outright fraud to steal it away.

The supposed surrender of the Haldimand Tract was an optical illusion orchestrated by Canada. It would appear that land was surrendered because there are signatures on the document. Look close enough, however, and you see the magician wasn't really a magician at all, but a con artist.

During a secret meeting between a small number of chiefs and Canada, the few Confederacy chiefs were led to believe that they had no power to stop the building of Plank Road over the Haldimand Tract, today known as Highway 6. Seven people at that meeting supposedly signed a surrender. Yet, one of the signatories was not a chief, and one of the chiefs claimed he was never at the meeting to begin with. His signature seems to have been forged. Regardless, the five valid chiefs' signatures were not even close to the fifty required for any agreement to be good. In addition, the money agreed to in the supposed surrender was never accounted for.

The idea that Canada did all of this is horrible, but truth is hardly pretty.

The O.P.P. promised us they would not put together a surprise attack on our camp. They promised they would notify us before coming in. Then they launched a surprise raid on our land reclamation site at 4 a.m.

My older brother was beaten by those police. Crimson and violet bruises mark his body like gravestones. The police picked him off the ground by his collar, choking him unconscious. When he came to, he was in a jail cell.

Fifteen others were taken to jail with him, all in varying degrees of pain and injury, but the police brutality never made it to any mainstream media reports.

What did get media attention was the method we used to signal our brothers and sisters on Six Nations that we were in distress: burning tires. The way we chose to ensure the safety of the rest of the camp, blockading the roads, was all that any non-Native saw.

"A horrible inconvenience," the residents of Caledonia call our protest. I am unsure how many tears they shed finding out that tires were being burned for three hours. I don't know how their lives have been changed forever by our causing a ten- minute road detour.

I do know that I cried for hours after finding out my brother was one of those attacked while I was at home sleeping. I know that he has a criminal record now for trying to correct an injustice done to our people years ago. I know that I don't remember what it was like to go grocery shopping with my mother in Caledonia without being afraid. Still, their unfeeling eyes burn into me from across the barricade. Things will never be the same.

GOOD CHILD
by Tony Liske

THE YEAR WAS 1921 AND summer was here. Geese were in. The Little Indian boy lived in Old Fort Rae with his family, and he had a grandfather, a mother and a drum. The Little Indian boy's name was Chekoa Neze meaning "good child."

His grandfather was old and wise and his name was Big Pierre. He was tall with big whiskers. He was born in this land in 1883. He had been here a very long time. He had very bad hearing, so bad that sometimes he couldn't even hear what Chekoa Neze was saying.

Chekoa Neze rarely saw his grandfather, because his grandfather worked a lot out on the trapline at Trout Rock. When Chekoa Neze came home from school for lunch, his mother had caribou all boiled up for him. And when he came home after school, his mother had dried meat all ready for him. When his grandfather came back from the bush, he was tired and went right to bed.

His mother was a special person. She was someone with whom he was always safe, especially when he was scared or hurt. Chekoa Neze loved her very much, but sometimes he would forget to tell her and when he realized it, he used to run and find her and give her a kiss on the cheek. "What a loving boy he is," said grandfather.

Chekoa Neze loved to play outside with his drum made of caribou skin. In the winter, grandfather made the drum with his big hands and showed Chekoa Neze how to play it. This made grandfather very happy.

One day, grandfather said to him, "Big meeting coming tomorrow, I want you to come with me Chekoa Neze." He was happy. Holding grandfather's big hand and going to this big event was a special time for him.

Chekoa Neze ran to his mother and told her the good news, and she told him to take his drum, too.

Chekoa Neze went in his room and started cleaning his drum with caribou fat to make it shiny for the big day. He took out his church clothes and laid them on his wooden chair by his bed, so when he got up in the morning they would be all ready for him. He was happy because he could play his drum at the big meeting with his grandfather. Chekoa Neze wanted to sing and play the drum like his grandfather.

Grandfather had a good life in the bush. His father taught him to live good and how to survive in the bush. His mother taught him to cook and respect the land of the Dene People. And grandfather wanted the same good life for Chekoa Neze.

After Chekoa Neze finished with his drum, he went outside to help grandfather carry the wood inside. Grandfather stopped and looked at Chekoa Neze and told him, "Tomorrow special men are coming to our village to talk about land, and then we are going to sign our names on the paper so our children can have a good life." Checkoa Neze did not understand why special men wanted to talk about this land when it was already theirs. He was thinking how the old grandfathers used to talk about how they needed to take care of their land and pass it on to their children to take care of. Chekoa Neze wanted to learn more about land.

The next morning, the sun shone brightly with clear blue skies. Grandfather came into Chekoa Neze's room and gently woke him up whispering softly into his ear that it was time to go. Chekoa Neze jumped out of bed and changed into his church clothes ready for the big day. He ran to his mother, held her for a long time and said, "Mother, today is a big day for me and time for me to go."

Grandfather and Chekoa Neze ate rabbit soup for breakfast with fish egg bannock that mother made before she went to bed. It was good and tasty, grandfather's favourite soup.

Grandfather grabbed Chekoa Neze's hand and went out the door to the big meeting, which was held in a big white tent by the lake. As they were walking to the big tent, grandfather's old friends and family were walking the same way. There were lots of people. Chekoa Neze saw many of his friends, too.

The white tent seemed so big. He saw four men wearing red, black and yellow clothes waiting outside the tent. They each carried a gun. Inside, he saw an old man with white skin sitting behind a table. He had on a black coat and in his hand was a small skinny black stick. He had white paper in front of him on the table. Beside him sat two younger men with white skin wearing black. Behind them was Bishop Breynant from Fort Providence. *I remembered him, how he would sometimes come to our school and talk about God in our language. I was so happy to see him,* thought Chekoa Neze. Chekoa Neze tugged on the grandfather's hand because he wanted to know who those special men were.

Grandfather looked down at Chekoa Neze and said, "Yes, my Chekoa Neze?"

Chekoa Neze said, "Who are these men, Grandfather?"

Grandfather stroked his big whiskers and smiled and said, "The old white man sitting down holding the pen is the Treaty Inspector, Conroy and the two men are his assistants. And of course, behind is the Bishop Breynant with some of his missionary friends. Finally, the four holding guns are the North West Mounted Police who travel everywhere with them. They are here to help with our land for hunting and trapping. They are here to help protect what is ours. These are called treaty rights, my son."

Chekoa Neze shrugged and looked around. He saw many Indian people sitting on the grass waiting for their turn to sign their name on the big white paper. On the other side of the tent, Chekoa Neze could hear drumming and laughing. He let go of grandfather's hand and ran towards the sound of the drumming and laughing. As he got closer, he could see there was a big gathering of white people and Indian people around. The old and the young were playing hand games. This was a funny game. It was like playing hide-and-seek with singing and laughing. The drums started rolling and the old chanting song began. The Song they were singing was of their land and animals. The men started hiding their sticks under the caribou hide and singing and drumming at the same time. The game could last for a short time or a long time. I looked around and the people were happy and laughing. I was happy.

I ran back to grandfather and he was signing his name on the white paper. I stood beside him as I watched the special men smiling and thanking grandfather for signing the paper. As we slowly made our way from the table, I grabbed my drum from grandfather's belt and started softly drumming the land song. I knew at that moment, that this day was the day of sorrow and happiness. I knew my grandfather was happy but was quiet for he knew this was the start of new beginnings for me. This land was ours and would always be ours. I ended the Song and then my grandfather picked up his drum and joined the other grandfathers singing in victory and triumph over this land!

A DAY OF HEALING
by Nicholas Printup

The sun began to set and all was calm across the lake. The boy, gazed into the shimmering light that reflected off the water, would now take his only rest upon a fallen tree before he reached his destination. The boy would wait until night before he moved, and as night came, so went the boy. Running and running through the bush, sure to stay clear of any roads or paths and taking no time to rest, the boy grew weary. Though gasping for air on every breath, the boy knew he could and would not stop, just as he was told to do. Just as the boy felt as though he would faint, morning light broke through the clouds. The boy had not yet reached his destination but was relieved to get some rest.

The boy fell onto his stomach, lying in the dewy grass. He could now rest and was grateful for that, but the fear and anxiety he had built up over the course of the night overwhelmed his soul. The boy lay in the grass panting, reminding himself over and over again what he had been told to do. He was reminded of everything that had taken place the last few days and prayed to the creator for strength. The boy wondered to himself why it was that his mother had acted the way she did. He knew she loved him more than anything in this world, but he could not make sense of the occurrences over the last two days. He did, however, know that whatever was happening had to do with the white woman in the green dress.

She had driven up to the house in a new black Buick, a material luxury his family would never own. When she stepped out of the car, the boy, his sisters and mother watched on from within the house. The white woman in the green dress walked through the broken fence and abruptly knocked on the front door. The boy's mother answered the door and kindly invited the woman in. The white woman in the green dress told the boy's mother that she was from social services and was there to talk about the children. The boy's mother told the boy and his sisters to go play outside. The children did as they were told but watched in the window from outside in an attempt to hear the conversation that the white woman and their mother were having. The children realized that they could not hear anything of what was going on in the house; they could only watch. It seemed to the children that the white woman in the green dress was upsetting their mother. The boy's mother began acting erratic towards the white woman and soon chased the woman out of the house. The white woman in the green dressed left in a calm manner looking back at the boy's mother before getting into the Buick and saying, "There's nothing that can be done; we'll be taking him soon enough." The boy's mother screamed in rage at the woman and told the woman to leave. It was right after that when the boy noticed his mother began to act differently.

The boy had finally caught his breath and quickly rose to his feet. He looked around at his surroundings and tried to construct a plan. The boy could hear the river flowing close by and his thirst lead him toward the river. When he got to the river the boy immediately jumped in. The water felt like silk against the boy's skin and every gulp the boy swallowed, enabled him to regain his composure. After having quenched his thirst and bathing the night's sweat off, the boy found a thickly covered area of bushes and trees where he could not be found, just as he was told to do. Once again, he would wait until night before he moved. The boy, again, tried to make sense of what had happened and went over what he was told to do.

Once the white woman in the green dress had driven out of sight, the boy's mother grabbed him by the hand and pulled him into the shed, slamming the door solidly behind them. She tried to speak, but the tears from her eyes flowed so constantly that her hands were too busy wiping them away. At every word she tried to speak, her voice sounded as though she was being strangled. Clearly something was wrong, the boy had never seen his mother cry this way before. The boy's mother was finally able to calm herself to a point where she could talk to her son. She looked at him and told him that social services had labelled her an unfit parent. The boy, unaware of what this term meant was confused. His mother explained to him that he had to leave if he wanted to keep living with her and his sisters. His mother also explained that if he did not go, he would be sent to the Mush Hole. The boy did not know much about the Mush Hole, but what he did know made him feel sick to his stomach. He had several friends and family members that had been sent to the Mush Hole as children. The boy knew that social services scooped up a lot of children on the reserve and had been doing so for sometime. He also knew that when they were sent to the Mush Hole, they did not come back until years later when they were all grown up. He was, then, told the instructions he was to carry out. His mother told him that he was to go to the lake and wait until night to move with the goal of reaching his grandmother's house, where it was safe. During the day, he was to hide and rest. When he reached his grandmother's, he was to stay put and wait until someone came to get him.

    Night fell and the boy knew he had not much further to go. He got up and began running to his grandmother's house. He seemed to feel a lot better than the night before. The feelings of anxiety and fear were gone and all that was left was the anticipation for what would come next. He could now see the smoke from his grandmother's chimney in the night's air, which acted as a better guide than his limited sense of direction. When the boy cleared the treeline, his face lit up with relief and cheer at the sense of his accomplishment. He had made it to his grandmother's house and done as he was told. He could now stop running, rest and wait until someone came for him. As the boy proceeded to walk towards the front of the house, he once again saw the new black Buick with the white woman who was wearing the green dress standing nearby. The boy's face soon lost its radiance and fell towards the ground like an overhead bombing. He heard his name cried many times from the porch. As he turned his head to see, he was suddenly picked up off his feet and shoved into the back of the Buick. From the back of the car he could see that it had been his grandmother calling his name but was being held back by a man in her attempts to help her grandson. The boy had not fought the man that had picked him up and tossed him into the car like a bag of garbage because he was exhausted from his journey. All he could do was watch out the back window as the car drove off down the road with his grandmother chasing behind it in desperation. A tear rolled down the boy's chin clearing a line of dirt from his face, as he knew he would not see his family for sometime or never again – a truth that he knew he had to endure.

***

Awakened, the boy, now an old man. He was at first disoriented as to his whereabouts. He looked to his right from which the nudge that woke him came. There sat another old man, much like himself, holding an eagle feather and motioning to pass it to the boy. The boy looked around the room and found that he was seated in a circle of many people, and the soothing aromas of Sweet Grass and Sage filled the atmosphere. He realized that there was a flip chart in the middle of the circle, which read "<u>WELCOME RESIDENTIAL SCHOOL SURVIVORS: A Day of Healing</u>." He now knew where he was and why. The boy reached for the feather in a hesitant manner, with his hand shaking, wishing that he was reaching instead for the bottle he left at home in the top cupboard to escape this reality. The boy grabbed hold of the feather but remained silent gazing into the space as if it were the shimmering light that was reflected off the water when all was calm.

ECHOES OF TAMARACK
by Candace Brunette

The persistence of memory lies in survival.
In a moment where stillness and silence
give voice to warm soft winds blowing
whispering words that guide craftsman to listen.

Today locals exhibit tiny treasures
carefully laid out on portable folding tables
set up in anticipation for the 4 o'clock train.

Across the gravel road
water taxis transport people
boarding at the clay banks
bringing back and forth
from island to mainland.

The moisture in the air
releases vapours from its oily pores
woody musk like scents
surface in the wind.

Aromas persuade us to notice
its burnt orange and russet brown tones
highlighted by the rays of the sun.

These swamp babies are gathered seasonally
when branches shed deciduous pine needles
revealing scaly egg like cones.

Gummy sap seeps from its bark
and tastes delicious on our tongues.
Its roots are used to bind and tie together.
Inner bark cleanses and purifies
moving our inner worlds.

These bunches of tamarack branches
are fused together
telling stories of survival
past and present
forming miniature bird like creatures
with no wings to fly.

Across the craft table
tourists admire them
imagining the pretend birds
as decoration in their lavish homes
soaring from their ceilings
nestled on their coffee tables.

They imagine them
even though yesterday
tamarack birds were used
as life size decoys to hunt.

Today
they still feed our families.

WILD FLOWERS
by Kerissa M. Dickie

Rose opened her eyes to the sight of a great building. The bus pulled up and parked alongside, and she looked up at the wall of windows and brick in astonishment. Lights all along the exterior of the first floor lit the building, throwing light up high to the third floor. The school was alive in its size. It made the sky seem like a puddle. She sat up straight, and wriggled her cold toes and fingers. The 10 hours in the poorly heated bus, and its climb higher and higher into the mountains had filled her stomach and head with nausea. As she stepped off the bus, in a line herded by the bus driver, she pulled her eyes away from the school and scanned the grounds. Tall, untended grasses and weeds stretched towards thin forest and were coated in the night's frost. Darkness and dim nothing touched the horizon.

Rose clutched onto the sack her mother had given her before boarding the bus, and used it to block the cold wind from her throat. There was dry meat and bannock inside, and the canvas still held onto the bitter, musky smell of porcupine quills and moose hair.

Settled into a hard cot that night, Rose listened to other girls chatter in the darkness. Some spoke Cree, but most spoke Slavey, and she listened to them make jokes about the nuns in their stuffy dresses. Rose listened to the wind wrestle with the large windows at the end of the room. She tried to stay as still as she could, and squeezed her thighs together. They had been ordered to urinate before bed, but the stalls and crowd of strangers in the bathroom had made her bladder lock up tight in self-consciousness. Now it was ready to burst, and she was using all of her energy to will it away. She let her breath out in tiny wisps into her pillow.

Hours later, Rose awoke to the shrill sound of a bell and realized she had wet the bed. Humiliation pounded through her ears. When she refused to stand up, Sister Florence wrenched her out of bed and discovered the mess. Instead of having breakfast, she was stripped naked in the shower room. Rose shook with cold, and stared at the tiled wall. She sputtered against the water that fell from the ceiling above her — it was colder than any rain she had known, and it tasted metallic. The sister forced a bar of soap into her hand and gestured for Rose to rub it into every part of her body. It smelled like moose fat. She closed her eyes and imagined her mother's smokehouse flooding with water.

***

It was a bitterly cold November afternoon, and Louis was waiting for his turn to play stick hockey on the ice rink in the boys' yard. He paced along the fence, running his stick along the open grooves. The loud, grating noise of it satisfied his frustration.

"*Senándeh!*" A girl yelled from the other side of the fence.

She was sitting on the girls' side of the fence on the edge of a snow bank with her teeth bared in a grimace. Her hair was cut into a short bob that grazed her earlobes, the style forced onto all girls at school, and her honey-brown cheeks were blotchy with cold. Her lips, sitting open, were topped with a perfect cupid's bow. She turned her back to him and went back to fidgeting with something on the ground between her legs. Louis leaned into the fence.

"Sorry." He needed for her to turn around. "What you doing?" He needed to look at her face again.

"Get lost, you crazy bush Indian." She swatted in his direction.

Louis felt a giggle rise from his chest, and his stomach relaxed into a lazy puddle.

He was happy to be anything she wanted to call him. "What's your name?"

"Rose. Why?"

"I'm Louis." Everything about her felt like a book being read. Something someone had to have written about already. She had dark eyes and cheekbones sitting high in chubby cheeks. "You need help with something?"

Rose's face grew soft. "Could you teach me how to make fire?" She showed him a handful of broken twigs. Her fingertips and palms looked raw. "I'm trying, but nothing is happening."

"*Ná*." He held his hand out towards her, and she stuck the twigs through the squares of the fence and into his palm. He rubbed one between his fingertips. "What do you need fire for?"

"If I'm going to make it all the way back home, I'll need fire to keep me warm."

"You're going home?"

"I tried to get into the storage room with all our stuff from home. You know the coats and gloves they took from us? But it's locked. So it's even more important for me to learn how to make fire to keep warm."

Louis lowered himself onto his haunches, and rested his elbows on his knees.

"Well, I know how to make fire. I could teach you."

A smile shot across her face and she scooted herself right close to the fence. She leaned forward. "Or you could just go with me. Tonight's movie night, so everyone will be in the basement. We can sneak out and just follow the highway out of the mountains."

Hunched over, on the other side of the fence, Louis realized that he was close enough to smell her. Her icy breath fogged into his face. It smelled like soup, mixed in with a smell of oily, flowered soap that he imagined must come from her hair. It was the best smell in the world. The idea of wrapping himself around her made him feel his heartbeat in his pelvis. "Is your town very far?"

***

While a projector roared in the basement, illuminating a room full of rapt faces, Louis was layering socks. His own pair, marked with his identification number 19, was the first layer of three other pairs he stole from the dirty laundry. He used his wool blanket as a sack, and he filled it with extra clothes, paper for kindling and crusted bread and beans that he saved from dinner. He was growing more and more nervous, thinking of the cold winter air outside and the darkness they would walk through.

He walked softly down the stairs, with his breath held in his chest. Each impulse to go back, empty his sack, and crawl into bed was drowned out by a new and vibrant image of Rose sitting across from him.

"Young man!" A high voice screeched, just as the lock on the front door knob clicked open. The door was stuck with ice around the edges. The nun yanked hard on the back of his coat, and it knocked the breath out of him.

***

Rose wasn't at morning Mass. No one had seen her. The entire day stretched like a path through muskeg. Louis' feet dragged and he had to struggle to keep himself standing straight. During afternoon mass, Louis listened to the Father drone on, and felt his muscles flexing and jumping in panic against the cold wood of the pew. He focused on the shaved head of a boy in the row in front of him. He watched a single louse cross his skull in a slow, steady path from one side of his head to the other.

The door to the chapel opened right after Holy Communion, just as the last pews of students returned to their seats. Sister Florence hurried to the front of the chapel. She whispered something to Father David, and his face blanched in reaction.

"Children, stay in your seats." Father David was a balding French man with thick glasses. He followed the nun out of the room.

Louis stood up and made his way to the chapel door, almost tripping on the kneeling post. He peered into the hall and followed the sound of voices coming from upstairs. He sat near the top of the staircase, peeking through the banisters. Father David and the Sister were huddled by the front door, along with Mr. Galibois, the Indian Agent.

"RCMP got the call two hours ago. A trucker saw her on the road, a few miles from here. Sent me to handle it." Mr. Galibois' voice was raspy, but soft in the middle. "Should I take her to the hospital in town?"

Louis placed his hands in his lap and stared blankly at the bundle of cheek and blanket lying at their feet.

"There's nothing that can be done now. You have to take her to her family. Bring her home." Louis could see the side of her face. Her skin was pale, as if she had been rubbed just slightly with dust, and her lips were pursed shut.

Everything seemed to stop then.

Louis was sent to a different residential school the next fall. It was over a thousand miles from the fence and his conversation with Rose, but no farther than a night of sleep without dreams of her.

***

A newborn whimpers and squirms in her tight papoose of a hospital blanket. "Shhh. Momma's trying to sleep, Rose." Louis reaches for her in his sleeping wife's arms, grasps her under the shoulder and bum, and draws her to his chest. He cradles the baby into his armpit, lets the feathery weight of her rest on one arm and curls the other arm around her. She has slanted eyes, tiny rounded nostrils and a little bow atop thin lips. A tuft of dark hair swirls on top her head and her skin is a soft pink. He loosens one arm free from the fleece blanket and sprawls out her hand with his index finger. Tiny fingernails catch hold of the deep lines and rough texture of his skin. Water runs across the smooth film of his eyes. He blinks, and tucks the blanket back around her arm.

Louis walks slowly to the window and looks out into the hot, July afternoon. The Maternity Ward is on the second floor, at the back of the hospital, and a field of grass sits below. Bumblebees and a dragonfly flutter past the window; one hits the pane with a little tap and buzzes back on its way. Patients, in crisp hospital robes, smoke on benches placed near king-size beds of yellow flowers. They squish their cigarette butts into a tin ashtray with a twist, and squint through the sunlight at one another as they speak. He focuses on a barbed-wire fence in the distance that separates the hospital lot from a forest grove. It's old and bent forward: its top rung reaching toward the weeds.

Louis closes his eyes and imagines drifts of snow washing across the window sill. Heavy, brilliant white packs down the field grasses below and weighs down the tree tops. A young girl appears through the haze of swirling snow. She swings a canvas sack, back and forth, and stops to smile at him. Her eyelashes and the hair framing her face are frozen into crystals. Her cheeks are perfect circles of pink. She gives him an impatient wave with her glove and motions for him to hurry. Then she is swallowed by a flurry of snow, and the frozen world outside begins to melt at the edges as his lids open.

"Rose," Louis looks into the newborn's face. "I promise to teach you everything I know."

SILENCE SPEAKS A THOUSAND WORDS
by Amanda Wapass-Griffin

A CROWD OF ANGRY, JEERING spectators had gathered, driven out of their warm homes by their self-righteous need to see these savages die. The papers had printed the grisly details over and over about the Frog Lake massacre the past spring and the people were crying for justice.

Wandering Spirit stood tall, seemingly unhindered by the shackles around his hands and feet. His face held no emotion as he looked out over the crowd of spectators. He was unafraid of the hatred painted on the faces of those before him. He looked down on them, and he felt pity. *How could they understand the plight of his people? How could they understand that he had been fighting for the survival and the future of his children? Wouldn't they have done the same?*

He slowly closed his eyes, trying to block out the icy chill that penetrated every pore of his weary body. He allowed his mind the luxury to drift back to another time and place. He had been a young man once, his body muscled and lithe, his eyes dark and piercing. The stories, whispered in hushed awe around crackling fires, told of the many Blackfoot he had killed, more than any other warrior in his band. The chief had once given Wandering Spirit a bonnet made of an entire lynx pelt, wrapped until head and tail met, adorned with five eagle plumes. He had worn it proudly. To him, it was a symbol of his ability to protect his people. To others, it evoked awe and fear.

Wandering Spirit breathed in a long, shaky breath and the memories of a life that once was drifted into his mind. He remembered standing on a grassy hill near his people's camp, the tall grass gently swaying around his legs, the cacophony of birds and insects filling the silence, and the warmth of the midday sun embracing him. He remembered looking out over the gentle roll of the hills that stretched on endlessly. They seemed alive as the prairie grass that covered them moved in waves up and over the hills, dancing to the orchestra of the wind. Wandering Spirit breathed in deeply, certain he could smell the richness of that prairie soil, still damp from morning's heavy dew. How he loved the land.

He was jarred back to reality when he heard Bad Arrow speaking in a hoarse whisper. *Was it already time for their last words?* He hadn't heard what the first two men said. Bad Arrow's voice rose as he continued to pray to the Creator for his family. Wandering Spirit knew Bad Arrow was thinking about the young son he would leave behind and to what end?

Wandering Spirit closed his eyes again trying to shut out the fathomless gray in the scene that surrounded him, and he silently sent up his own prayer to the Creator: *Do you hear me? Do you feel how my heart aches for my people and not for myself? I have accepted this death prepared for me. I only ask that you protect my people. Watch over them, Great Spirit, as the journey ahead of them will be long and hard.*

Unbidden whispers of a life that once was filled his mind. He saw a group of about 20 tipis, standing like proud pinnacles on the expanse of the prairie, thin threads of smoke acting as spires as they trailed into the sky. He could see racks of bison meat drying in the sun. It had been a successful hunt, and his people were preparing the meat, a process that would take weeks. He could see children running between tipis, laughing, as their mothers scraped the bison hides.

There was a sudden sharpness in his chest at the memory. How strong and proud his people had been. It seemed so long ago and yet the memories remained strikingly clear. Life had changed so quickly, the change had spread like a prairie fire leaving behind a charred and seemingly lifeless landscape.

Wandering Spirit remembered standing among his people, their tipis showing sign of wear. The women had tried to patch the worn bison hides as best as they could, but weakness from hunger had stripped them of their vitality and strength. The atmosphere around the camp was solemn and the tension stifling. People moved about the camp, their shoulders slumped and their faces drawn.

He had gone to see Chief Big Bear, already an old and tired man, to plead with him to allow Wandering Spirit, war chief, and his warriors to do something, anything. The chief told him that there had been talk that bands in the east had made treaties with the government, surrendering their land for promises of a new way of life. The chief's voice had been sombre and that night, in the shadows of firelight, Wandering Spirit noticed the deep lines that etched age into the chief's face. He knew the chief did not want trouble with the white man. He also knew that the chief remained wary of the promises they made in these treaties. When it came time to meet with the government, Wandering Spirit had stood behind the chief when he refused to leave his mark on that piece of paper that promised his starving people life again in exchange for their freedom.

Wandering Spirit shivered and shifted his weight. The boards beneath his feet felt cold and strange, and he yearned for the softness of the earth. Little Bear began to speak his last words, his raspy voice crying out in anguish about the plight of their people and the desperation that had driven them to make a stand. Wandering Spirit knew the desperation that Little Bear spoke of instantly. When the chief had left that gathering with the government, the paper still missing his mark, Wandering Spirit had felt a surge of hope. Maybe, now, the chief would listen to him. His heart ached to fight back instead of waiting for hunger and weakness to overcome him and his people. His warriors had done what they could to overpower the hunger that had clawed at the peoples' empty bellies.

They had set up camp on the Frog Lake Reserve, near Fort Pitt, the autumn before, and the previous winter had not been easy on the haggard and wearied people. Many succumbed to the death that they had been fighting off so valiantly. Wandering Spirit's band had travelled from the plains of Montana where they had come back starving and empty-handed.

Wandering Spirit and his warriors had spent that exhausting winter snaring rabbits and other small game, distributing the meagre portions among the people. Some took it with a fleeting look of gratefulness in their sunken eyes while others, their flesh hanging on their bones, remained curled up inside their tipis too weak to even notice. He had gathered all that he could find of value in the camp that could be spared and had taken it to the store on the settlement nearby to trade for food.

Wandering Spirit felt his body tense as he remembered what Thomas Quinn, the Indian Agent, had scornfully told him, "No work, no food." He knew Quinn was suggesting that the chief needed to put his mark on the paper if he expected anything from the government. He had walked away from Quinn that day empty-handed. But, as his people grew weaker, Wandering Spirit's rage had grown stronger until it burned in him like a powder keg ready to explode.

Iron Body was crying out in anger now, his words sharp and condemning. Though the people who had gathered to watch him die, would not understand his words, his tone conveyed his anguish. Wandering Spirit couldn't help but steal a sideways glance at the brave warrior that he had fought beside almost all his life. Iron Body's face was contorted with rage, his eyes shut tight, and his face pointed towards the sky. Wandering Spirit noticed, for the first time the long thick ropes that hung like dead weights behind each man. Wandering Spirit's stomach tightened, and he felt Iron Body's angst as if it was his own.

Even as his own stomach gnawed in hunger, and his body grew weaker, Wandering Spirit approached the chief, hell-bent on being heard.

"We need to stand up and fight or we will soon be too weak to do anything but curl up and die. No more waiting. The people are desperate and the warriors restless."

The chief had listened to him in silence, his craggy face remaining emotionless and Wandering Spirit remembered feeling sorry for him. It was at that moment that Wandering Spirit had realized it was up to him to do something and that he had to make the next move. He was the raw chief, after all. He had gathered his warriors on that sunny, cloudless spring day, and they headed for the Frog Lake settlement.

Miserable Man's final war cry, feared in the heat of battle, echoed in sharp contrast to the sombre scene before them. Wandering Spirit saw Thomas Quinn's face again. He and his warriors had come to the settlement to try to get food for the starving people. But Quinn refused to cooperate. Even with a gun trained on him, Quinn sneered at Wandering Spirit and his warriors with contempt and superiority and tried to grab Wandering Spirit's gun. Quinn was quick and strong but misjudged the distance between him and the gun. The shot sounded like an explosion and Quinn's face contorted in a look of sheer surprise as the bullet tore into his body. Wandering Spirit remembered Quinn's body falling hard to the ground and then standing over the man who had wielded so much power over the destiny of his people. He had watched his blood pour out onto the earth, somehow knowing that in that moment he had lost his life, as well. Eight more men had died after Quinn that day, and still his people went hungry.

The man beside him began to sing, pulling Wandering Spirit from his memories. Walking in the Sky's last song stirred the warrior's heart. He exhaled and his body slumped forward slightly; his shackles suddenly unbearably heavy. After Walking in the Sky, he was the only man whose last words remained unspoken.

His heart cried for his people and he saw them as they were – strong and resilient, and Wandering Spirit knew they would survive. They would find a way to stand proud again. He opened his eyes and saw the sea of people looking up at him expectantly, waiting to hear what this last man had to say before the rope was put over his head and he breathed his last.

Suddenly there was a break in the clouds and a single beam of sunlight beckoned. Wandering Spirit stood tall, imagining he was wearing his war bonnet and holding his bow and arrow, his body strong again. He felt the gentle breeze of the prairie wind on his body and the sweet smell of sage and sweetgrass in his nostrils. His words dissipated in the sunlight. Wandering Spirit closed his eyes, the strength of his ancestors coursing through his body. He had not felt the rope around his neck, heavy and chafing. His burden had lifted. It did not matter what he said. His last words were embodied in the life he had lived.

On November 27, 1885, eight men were hanged in Battleford in Canada's largest mass execution in history. Six of the men: Broken Arrow, Little Bear, Iron Body, Miserable Man, Walking in the Sky and Wandering Spirit, were hanged for their involvement in the death of nine men at Frog Lake on April 2, 1885; the other two for an unrelated incident. Of the six, Wandering Spirit was the only one that had no final words. Yet his spirit lives on in each one of us as we continue to fight, not with words but with our lives, for the future of our children and our grandchildren. *Eksoi.*

THE ENCHANTED OWL
by Jessica Yarrow

THE ARTIST'S HANDS ARE NIMBLE. Her dark eyes are focused and caring. As her fingers guide the smoky lead of the pencil, her mind is streaming the flood of ideas and images that fill her head. As the swirls and shades on the paper begin to engulf the white emptiness of the canvas, a lifetime of memories that influenced her now shape the birth of an owl. The first lines are timid, marking where the sketch will begin, and where the sketch will end. She sweeps the lead delicately, with the precision of a trained hand. She hums a few notes, in no particular order, just as they come to her. The sketch is similar to her tune, emerging from the pencil as the image appears in her mind, no reason or method explained. She knows she wants to create an owl. Birds are a fond subject for her. She never knows what shape they will take; she just focuses on pleasing her eye with a pleasant yet capturing image. Her focus sinks deeper into the shapes and contours of the owl's tail as her mind wanders through her life, and what has brought her to this moment, creating this new image of life.

As the sketch continues to take the shape of a wise and beautiful owl, the artist thinks about her own birth and the elements of her own existence that are shaping the creature before her. She was born in 1927 in Ikerrasak, and vividly remembers her first experiences with drawing. Early in her twenties seemed an unusual age to start what many people began as children. Her art started as a way of passing the long hours of the day while she recovered from a battle with tuberculosis, but she loved this new expression of creativity she had discovered. Art became her; she became art. She was talented in a way no one had seen before. Her images, although simple to the eye, were constantly explored deeper, to find their true meaning. She gained respect as an artist quickly. She remembers the connection she had with Johnniebo, a fellow artist, and the man she would eventually marry. They shared a great love of art and she fondly recalls the many days spent stone carving and drawing together. She and Johnniebo had met a creative and intelligent man, by the name of James Houston. It was James that encouraged them to experiment with shapes and colours, carving, and textures. He had a great influence on what would become her career, her passion, her life.

Swish swish swish…the comforting and familiar scratches of lead on paper make her smile as she thinks about drawings she has completed. She ponders what subject is her favourite. Is it birds? Humans? Spirits? The sun? Birds have always held a special place in her heart, yet to her, all animals, creatures, spirits and objects are valued and respected equally. She knows her community and art lovers alike especially admire her portrayal of majestic birds. She carefully outlines and fills in the owl's sharp talons and powerful feet. She begins the painstaking task of filling in the narrow spaces around the many specks of white on the body of the beast. She pays strong attention to detail, her lines and shapes all pleasing to one another. She adds suitable shapes to the image, not distracting from any particular element. It makes her smile to think of the happiness her drawings bring to people. As the mystical bird continues to fill the page, she considers it intriguing how the progression of a portrait is similar to her own growth as an artist. All drawings begin with an idea, a thought. The thought may be weak or blurry but over time becomes clear and confident. She too, has gone from a timid young artist to an accomplished and skillful master of expression and individualism. The artist alternates between the dark pencil and bold red shades she has chosen to create the portrait. She shades the transitions of colour in a way that is contrasting, but gradual. Her drawing stands out even more among the white paper, as the red and black create a dramatic likeness of the owl's figure. Her eyes are pleased with the image she is seeing, she smiles and continues etching along the page, filling the blankness with the beauty of this new creature.

The portrait is complete. The curves perfectly rounded, its shading flawless. Perfectly centred on the canvas, this new life stares back at its creator. She stares back at the beautiful creature, and with a breath of air as gentle as the hands that lined the page, she clears away the dusting of pencil left behind. What started as a few pale strokes on a backdrop of nothing, has transformed into a powerful image that startles the eye and touches the soul. She carefully places the drawing into a folder, next to the many other expressive portraits she has completed, not knowing the monumental effect it will soon have on her life. To her, the owl is just another portrait, significant to that particular moment in her life; she will later learn it is so much more.

Several months pass; the months turn to years. The owl still lies tucked away, safely surrounded by the spirit and vibrancy of many paintings, sketches and stone carvings. There have been many drawings since the owl, but the owl is always a favourite of onlookers. The viewers of the portrait are always captured by the striking contrast between the deep black and the vibrant red. Colour is a newer medium to her, although at a glance, the effects are superior, like she has been using colour for as long as she has known art. The shape of the tail feathers, the detailing on the body and the emotion in the eyes are the expressive detail true to the artist's signature style. She has great power as an artist, drawing two-dimensional images yet still having the ability to convey true emotion within those images. The owl leaves a lasting impression on its viewers, and will soon be unveiled to a wider audience, as wide as all of Canada.

The owl has been chosen. An image of great significance is chosen to be displayed to thousands of Canadians. She knows she has achieved a great success, simply doing what she loves. Expressing herself through art is a privilege she cannot imagine living without. She is humble yet pleased with her achievements, as she should be. She wants to be known by her art, not her name. Her art is now so well known that her name has also become recognized as one of great significance.

Kenojuak Ashevak is her name; she is proud to be the first Inuit woman to have her artwork grace a Canada Post stamp in the year 1970. Over her lifetime she will achieve an astonishing amount of recognition and success, dozens of honours many great Canadians only dream about. Her life will be documented in video, her name surrounded by dozens of other great Canadians on the Walk of Fame, and featured on several other Canadian stamps. Her art was not done for fame, for money or publicity. Her art was her own, a way of expressing the emotions that ran within her, depicting the experiences that touched her life and created the beautiful spirit of Kenojuak.

All she wanted to do was make something beautiful, and she did.

REMEMBER, MY GRANDSON, REMEMBER US
by Nicole Munro

Her frail hands worked tirelessly with the utmost care and attention on the beadwork for a pair of moccasins. They were for her grandson. They were a gift, a sort of parting gift. She knew she wasn't going to live much longer. Life was short, too short, and soon she would pass on.

Pausing, she reached for another bead, each one representing the concerns and thoughts that flooded her mind day after day as she watched her home — her world change — slowly before her eyes.

She was sitting underneath a small tree, situated in the shade, listening to the words of her Native language, and the words of the foreigners. A negotiation was taking place and all was quiet, every single person listening carefully, some leaning forward with anticipation. Chief Crowfoot stood in front, gesturing with his hands, clearly trying to get the foreigners, under a large tent, to comply with his demands. The Blackfoot hadn't been treated all that fairly in the past and Crowfoot was intent on changing that.

She had enough faith in her leader, but she strongly believed that this treaty would not change everything for the greater good. Slipping another bead onto a thread, her mind wandered.

Long ago, her ancestors lived off the land, with no restraints. Buffalo had been plentiful. Life had been long. They had been the only inhabitants of this land, including all other tribes.

Oh yes, they had their fair share of problems, mostly with the Cree, their enemies. But other than that, there had been no worries. Back then life was good. The Blackfoot had been feared and esteemed, a force to be reckoned with.

The world, in which the Blackfoot and all other Native tribes had lived, was changing, little by little, into something they all feared they would regret, something that would bring many calamities. Treaties were being signed. The government was afraid, she knew, of these people, the first residents of Canada. The government had quickly confined those in the East to reserves, limiting their food sources and way of life drastically.

She had heard of many false promises given to the Natives in the East. She had heard of injustice, of pain: both physical and emotional. The liquor that the foreigners had brought over was vile, destroying the lives of her people.

And finally, she had heard of the assimilation, the tradition and customs that had survived for countless decades, being stripped away, torn apart, and erased. All that once was, was quickly fading into nothingness, as if the Native Way had never existed.

Lifting her head, she listened as Crowfoot's voice floated across the grass. She wasn't too far away; she could hear his voice distinctly, the soon to be famous words echoing all around, soaring into every ear of every person present. Some were hopeful, some were unhappy. And some were just anxious to get a treaty going.

"Grandmother." A young voice broke her out of her reverie. She turned her head to see her twelve-year-old grandson approaching, intent on joining her under the tree. He was her only grandchild and he tried to spend time with her as much as possible. She wished she could see him every moment of the day, especially at this time in her life.

"What are you doing?" he asked.

She smiled, her deep brown eyes full of love and gratitude towards him for sitting with her.

"These," she said, indicating the beadwork with her free hand, "are moccasins, for you."

The boy grinned and reached out with one hand, fingers sliding across the beaded surface. "I do not know what I did to deserve these," he replied, glancing at the crowd, eyes lingering on a few of the older boys who had already done many things, great things in comparison to himself. "I long to go with my older brothers on raids, to be just like them," he added in a soft tone.

"Patience, my grandson," she chided gently, "patience. You will get there soon enough…" Her voice trailed off as the words of the foreigners reached her ears. "…If this treaty doesn't come to pass," she murmured bitterly.

The boy blinked. "What do you mean?"

Unwilling to share her worries, she changed the subject abruptly. "Promise me…" There was a slight pause. "Promise me you will always remember…us, the Blackfoot. Don't forget our way of life," she told him, gazing at him intently. "Remember the stories of your ancestors. Remember how life was good, when the buffalo roamed freely, in great numbers.

"Remember when the young men of our tribe earned their glory and prestige through horse raids, when they became warriors through our Sun Dance ceremony. Remember the stories told about acts of bravery.

"Remember the families, kept together by love and honour. Everyone respected one another and looked out for one another. Remember when we could do things without being held back by terrible disease.

"Remember when we hunted across the prairies to the east, and the foothills when we travelled west to the great rocks. Remember when we travelled north to the forest, and south to where the Long Knives have now taken over.

"Remember our Creator. Our people have always believed there was someone above us in the Great Sky, watching over us, now and forever. My grandson, the white father has told us there will be more of his people." He knew what she referred to. "Remember, my grandson, remember us."

Her grandson nodded, more determined to honor her wishes than ever. "I will not forget," he vowed solemnly.

She smiled and closed her eyes, salvaging that blissful moment in which her grandson promised to always remember. When her time came, she would go peacefully, resting at ease with the last knowledge of her mind being this moment.

The wind carried the last words of Chief Crowfoot. "…As long as the sun shines, the grass grows, and the river flows…" Crowfoot, she knew, was a wise man, and had made a wise manoeuvre in the signing of the treaty.

She opened her eyes and resumed her work once more. She chose the brightest beads and threaded them skillfully onto the moccasin. No more would each bead remind her of the problems. No, each bead in coming represented the hope she had for her grandson, and future generations of her family. Each bead would hold a little bit of memory and love, each one coming together in a delicate and elaborate design, portraying the work and effort she had put into raising her family.

Each bead would remind her grandson, whenever he wore them, of their conversation and the life that once remained.

Her frail hands worked tirelessly with the utmost care and consideration on the beadwork for her grandson's pair of moccasins.

MATERNAL TIES
by Sable Sweetgrass

When I graduated, back in 2011, from the Faculty of Law at the University of Calgary, I was wearing my family's elk tooth dress underneath a purple graduation robe. I had asked the grad committee if I would be able to wear the dress alone, but my request was denied.

I decided to wear it anyway, underneath their robe. Just before my name was called, I planned to slip off my shoes and put on my Grandma Annie's moccasins which were tucked under my arms, beneath the robes. My Grandma Annie was there, so was my mom and dad, and I had told them to look at my feet when I went up to accept my degree, so that they would know that underneath I had on the dress.

I sat there listening to the names being called out followed by the applause and camera flashes as each graduating student had their moment. My name, Mary Stands Alone, daughter of Pearling and Alex Stands Alone, was still far off and, so I pulled my right hand into the robe and I held the beaded and quilled amulet that hung from my neck. I let go and started stroking the hundreds of elk teeth sewn onto the midnight blue wool, feeling the rows and rows of smooth polished teeth running from the neck to the waist. I could imagine the pride my Great, Great Grandmother Appanii would have had wearing her dress.

Grandma tells me that Appanii gave her dress over to her daughter, Sikotan, when she came home from boarding school. For a woman, the elk tooth dress was a symbol of status and achievement, the more teeth, the more prominent, and the dress had hundreds. My Great Grandma Sikotan was the first person in our family to go to the boarding school and the first to speak English. Grandma says that her mom was to wear the dress to the Okan, the Sundance, that summer where it was held secretly. However, when her mom got home from the school she refused to put the dress on. What was worse was that Sikotan's baby cord amulet she had worn since birth was gone, taken away from her at the school.

My grandma says that her Mother Sikotan was a devout Catholic. The dress that Appanii tried to give her and the amulet that Sikotan would have worn throughout her life, were no longer of value to her in her new faith, new education.

My mom says that when she found the elk tooth dress at the Glenbow Museum 25 years ago, she also found Sikotan's amulet in a box containing dozens of other baby cord amulets. Sikotan's English name was tagged to both the dress and the amulet: Mary Theresa Wells. When mom pressed the amulet between her fingers, she could feel her grandmother and great grandmother's umbilical cord still inside.

Mom was a nurse's aide at the Indian Hospital in Cardston at the time. She went to the museum to physically assist the elders who were taken there to help the curators obtain more information on their Blackfoot artefacts. She said that the storage area was like a maze of wall-sized cabinets filled to capacity with the belongings of our people. Mom and the other people there to assist the elders, stood still and silent, as the curators opened one cabinet after another. They saw rattles, whistles, ceremonial clothing and headdresses, medicine shields, pipes and bundles. Cabinet after cabinet held more Kainai history: children's clothing, men's clothing, dolls, weapons, moccasins, tipis, story robes, winter coats, the list went on and on. Mom asked the curators where the elk teeth dresses were located. She said that as she and the curator approached the cabinets that held all these women's dresses, the doors of the cabinet were already open. Sikotan's dress was in there, in the first drawer Mom pulled out.

Mom stood by the dress, taking off the white gloves that were mandatory in the museum's collection area, and started counting all the elk teeth, running her fingers along the stitching, wanting so badly to put the dress on, to take it home. She found several strands of long gray hair stuck in the fastenings of the elk teeth and delicately placed them inside one of the white gloves, then placed the glove into her pocket.

One of the elders cried out that they had found their baby cord amulet and mom went over to her. In a long rectangular metal box lay dozens of amulets, one of them back around the neck of its owner. That elder who found them started pulling out the rest of them and reading out the few amulets that had names printed on them. One of the names was, Mary Theresa Wells.

Mom says that she returned to the cabinet that held her grandma's dress. There was an item card sitting next to it and she turned it over. The owner's name: Mary Theresa Wells was printed on it, as well as the person who sold it to the museum, Annie Crying Wolf.

***

My name would be called next. I took my Grandma Annie's moccasins from under my arms and dropped them to the floor. I removed my shoes with my feet and bent over to pull on the moccasins. "Mary Stands Alone," they called out and I stood up. I made my way toward the stage, the elk teeth under my robe clicking together with each step, people clapping and several camera flashes coming from the back of the auditorium where my mom and grandma were seated. I went up the seven steps to the stage floor and the president of the U. of C. who waited for me to accept my degree. I stopped and stood still for a moment.

It was my Grandma Annie who sold the dress to the museum. A decision that she tells me over and over will never stop hurting in her. It was a decision she had to make at that time in her life. Just out of boarding school, her Mother Sikotan and Grandma Appanii both passed away, she married my Grandpa John Crying Wolf at the age of 16. Grandma had inherited Sikotan's elk tooth dress and she says that she would wear it around the house all the time.

In those days, Grandma says there was more poverty and desperation. With four kids and another baby on the way, Grandma and Grandpa started selling off the few valuable things that they owned: livestock, farming equipment, furniture, and Sikotan's elk tooth dress.

It was a teacher and the priest from St. Mary's who brought the men from the museum over to my grandparent's place. They were bringing them around the reserve because these men were looking for things to put on display in their Banff museum. They saw my grandma wearing her dress as she served them the little food and tea they had in their cupboards and offered her $70 for her dress. Grandma says that the $70 she got was enough to get them by with food for another two winter months.

My mom never left that museum empty-handed. She and the elder who found the baby cord amulets would not leave without them. It was 1988 and the museum was getting ready to display their biggest exhibit of Aboriginal artefacts for the Calgary Olympics. That whole group of elders mom was with was upset and angry at what they had to leave behind and they all refused to leave without the two amulets. I guess the curators let them go, so as not to cause any controversy at the opening of their big exhibit. So they left, mom with Sikotan's amulet around her neck, and the elders determined to get back all of our ancestors belongings.

It seemed like forever that I stood on that stage at the top of the steps, but it was only a few seconds. It took me only a few seconds to make up my mind to do what I did. I took off my purple graduation robe, pulling it over my head to get it off. The clapping died down instantly and I could hear people talking and some people snickering. The robe was off and I hung it over my right arm in front of me and continued onto the podium. I stood next to the president and accepted my degree, taking it from her as she gave a faint, polite smile. I had on my family's elk tooth dress, though not the dress that was made for my Great Grandmother Sikotan, which was still locked up in the storage spaces of the museum. Instead, I was wearing the elk tooth dress that my mom and grandma had spent that past year making me. What I did have that belonged to my Great Grandmother Sikotan was the baby cord amulet. Inside it, Appanii and Sikotan's umbilical cord, were worn to keep the ties of Mother and Daughter strong.

THE UNKNOWN
by Réal Carrière

A PADDLE STIRS THE UNKNOWN, as a Father and Son discover a new river that was formerly unseen by man. Like all hunters, this Father understands the story of a broken leaf or the struggle behind yesterday's track. In an instant, he can visualise the thousands of beavers that have crossed the river, and he knows that he could feed his family for many weeks with the invisible life of this river. It is true that the beaver's lazy and industrious movements have been imbued deep into the images of his mind. They remind him of the movement of snow, a white snake's ghost whisper, drifting over the endless death of a winter lake. The Father took another stroke pushing the canoe deeper along the unknown and that was the exact moment when Columbus stepped onto the first beach of their "new world."

After a few seconds of paddling along the river, the Father knows that there are enough beaver to support a longer hunting expedition, possibly with his brother or his cousin. The time for that hunt is not now, as the Father knows he must return at that exact moment in order to arrive home before it is completely black. However, just before they left the river, the Father decided to quickly kill one beaver, so he could return home with a small showing of food. In no time, the Father harvested a beaver with the same technique that had been passed down for generations within his family. His family was known as great beaver killers; it was time to teach his son this simple and ancient technique. The Father was not worried about his son's young age because the Father had also learned at a young age his family's skill. After hundreds of years the skill, though crude in its origins, was his family's pearled speciality. So with the same amount of care as a Mother handling a child, the Father soon had a beaver in the canoe.

The Son, who recently turned eight, was fascinated with the beaver. Its belly was full. Its fur was brown and red. Its tail seemed masoned with a thousand black bones. Its claws were worn and full of wet river bottom earth. Its teeth were orange and one was partly broken. In the canoe, it seemed soft and full of water. On the ground, the Son knew it was slow yet like a rock. In the water, it was loud, quick, and clandestine, except for the trail of bubbles. The Father had paddled the canoe to the last portage and was out of the canoe when he told his son to bring the beaver out of the canoe.

At that place, the river was very narrow, but it was also very deep. The Son, though still a child, was not strong enough to carry the beaver without great effort. Mainly, he dragged the beaver on the edge of the canoe with its belly split between the world of the canoe and the water. Near the end of the canoe, only two steps from land, the Father momentarily took his hands from the canoe. The boat was suddenly unstable, and the Son dropped the beaver into the river. The Father started to laugh because his son quickly looked at him with an expression of fear and surprise, a look that the Father would never forget.

The Father was quite calm at that moment because he knew that with experience, the beaver would be floating and even if it were not there, it would only sink to the bottom of that small creek. His mood quickly changed when his son, without warning, disappeared into the river after the beaver. The Father quickly pushed the canoe aside and though he was slightly worried, he was still laughing. To the Father's surprise there was no movement in the water; it was as if his son had never jumped into the river. The Father waded into the water where his son would have entered. However, the Father discovered that the water was even deeper than he imagined, and though he tried to dive in to chase his son, he realized that his son had gone far deeper than even he could swim. Although the Father was worried, there was some hope in his heart because he knew that his family was also known for their exceptional swimming capabilities.

In the meantime, the Son was swimming after the beaver. At first, the river was dirty, but as the Son continued to swim, the water gradually became clearer until he could see the beaver also swimming, just a small way ahead. The Son would nearly reach the beaver when, with a quick movement of its tail, it would move slightly out of reach of the Son. Although the Son knew he loved to swim, he never knew that his natural ability would allow him to swim effortlessly and quickly.

After some time, the Son realized that instead of a watery silence he could actually hear the mumbles of distant voices. At first he assumed that it was the beaver, and then he realized that there were many voices, and that they all spoke with words that he could not understand. Listening very carefully, he began to recognize some of the words and he repeated these words because he thought that they were in the language of the beaver and that the beaver would understand. So he said, "Savage, king, god, gold, religion," but the beaver did not respond to any of those words.

Further on, the Son began to see more than the emptiness of the water. He saw images that he could not explain either but also images from his own life. First there were faces that he recognized like his mother, his sister, and his brother. Then there were moments like killing a squirrel, catching a fish with his hands, or laughing at his brother. Soon there were images that he did not understand like an old man telling stories to children, a woman he could not recognize, a river, trees, shiny rocks, colourful and strange hides, thousands of dead animals, tools that easily cut down trees, sandbars that extended as far as he could see, and a field of ice deep as the earth. In his struggle to reach the beaver, the Son thought that these images were the dreams of the beaver, so he started to tell the beaver everything he saw, so the beaver would understand that he understood the emotions of beavers. The beaver continued to swim and did not respond to anything that the Son said.

Eventually, the Son began to feel tired, but he knew that the beaver was also becoming tired because he was not losing any ground; this gave him renewed strength. However, he was also starting to lose his breath and knew that he would have to soon turn around to the surface. Soon after he started to think about his lack of breath, he knew that he would have to return to the surface. When he finally stopped, he realized that the beaver had taken him so deep that he did not know what direction the surface was. It seemed that every direction was as empty as the other; he knew that the search for the beaver was over, and the struggle for his life was about to begin.

When he looked towards the beaver, he realized that the beaver was also forced to make the same decision. Using that moment to his advantage, the Son grabbed the beaver. In excitement he said in Cree, "My father will be happy that I did not let the beaver get away, but I do not know which way is the surface." To his surprise the beaver also spoke Cree and said, "I know the way to the surface, but I do not have the energy to return. So if you have the energy, I will show you the way, provided you let me free when we reach the surface." The Son saw no alternative, so he accepted this proposition.

Working together, the water soon became murky and it was obvious that they were very near the surface. The moment before they reached the surface, the beaver said, "I have shown you the way; it is time to remember your promise. We have worked together, now you must let me go." The Son let go and just before he ran out of air, he broke the surface and faced his father. The Father did not smile, but he was happy.

The Son climbed to the shore and without speaking, they continued to cross the portage. The Father had made a fire, but knowing that they were close and that the Son would want to return home, he put out the fire. Eventually the Father's curiosity forced him to ask his son what he had seen beneath the water. After describing everything that he saw, the Son said, "I do not understand what I have seen. Can you help me?"

The Father replied, "I, also, do not understand but I know that what you have seen is called 'the unknown.' You will remember what you have seen today, and you will tell your children this story. Do not worry, my son. One day, everything you have seen will become known."

Cree word translations in the stories
Election Day and *My Brother Lonnie*

Kokum	Grandmother
Moshum	Grandfather

Slavey word translations in the stories
STEH-WAH and *Wild Flowers*

Etánana	You look beautiful
Mó	mom
Gá	rabbit
Elé	no
Babeha	baby
Heh	yes
Nedago	Nezu are you alright?
Senándeh	Shut up
Na	here take it

Writer Biographies

Candace Brunette
Candace is a 29-year-old woman of Omushkego Cree (people of the swamp land) and French-Canadian ancestry. Born and raised in Northern Ontario, Candace believes that her sense of home and intimate connection to land are central sources of inspiration in her writing. Her understanding of the body/spirit connection has deeply influenced and inspired her work. In 2007, Candace presented a piece of her second play, *Old Truck,* at Toronto's Waaseegachak Festival. A recent graduate of the Aboriginal Studies Program at the University of Toronto, she is currently enrolled in a master of education program. In her free time, she enjoys practicing and teaching yoga.

Cory Cappo
Cory is from the Muscowpetung Saulteaux Nation, and he was in Grade 12 attending Greenall School in Edenwold, Saskatchewan when he submitted his story *Election Day* in 2005 to the Our Story Challenge.

Réal Carrière
Réal is from the northern village of Cumberland House, Saskatchewan. Réal was raised on the trapline where he was home-schooled until Grade 10. For his final year of high school he was accepted to attend Lester B. Pearson College in Victoria and he stayed on the west coast until he finished his BA at Simon Fraser University. In the spring of 2006, Réal heard of the Our Story Writing Challenge so before leaving Vancouver he wrote an original story for this competition. Réal explains that, "In a small café I put my ideas together and this is the story (*The Unknown*) that is the result."

Chantelle Cheekinew

Sixteen-year-old Chantelle is from Regina, Saskatchewan. She loves writing, going to school and being with her family. And, like most teenagers, she also loves being with friends and going to the mall. Chantelle has had a passion for writing since she was in Grade four and is happy to say she inspires her family and friends. She thanks the Creator for her gift of storytelling and says she is ready for the challenges that lie ahead. Chantelle also submitted her story *My Brother Lonnie* in Cree to the Our Story Challenge, unfortunately due to time constraints the Cree version was omitted from this anthology.

Kerissa Marie Dickie

Kerissa was born and raised on the small Fort Nelson First Nation reserve of north eastern British Columbia. After graduating high school, she lived in Argentina for a year as a Rotary International Exchange Student, and returned with a new perspective of the world and of her identity as an Aboriginal person. She worked for her First Nation for a few years, in roles allowing her a wide range of experience, including working alongside the residential school survivors in her community and helping publish a book of their stories. Kerissa is now attending the University of Victoria as a writing student, and hopes writing will be a major part of her future. She credits her mother, Kathi, and grandmother, Adeline, as being her greatest sources of inspiration and strength.

Kelsea Northrop Donovan

A few years ago, Kelsea was hired by her band to be an assistant to the Residential School Healing Project. One of the project's goals was to create a book using a compilation of survivors' stories and artwork, a process that aimed to help in the healing process for each storyteller, to bridge the gap of understanding for younger generations, and to preserve a part of Aboriginal history that might otherwise be lost. Through reading their stories, Kelsea acknowledges the responsibility of being a member of the first generation not to go to residential school in her community. She notes that the stories of the survivors in her family and community have made a huge impact on the way she sees the world and on the kind of stories she wants to tell.

Alicia Elliott

Alicia has lived a migratory life, residing in various places around Turtle Island – across New York and Ohio, and most recently, the Six Nations Reserve. She is currently a second-year student at York University in Toronto, Ontario, where she studies English alongside her long-time partner, Mike Cannon. When she is not reading and cramming last-minute for class, she spends time in Brantford, Ontario with her darling daughter, Eva, or being lovingly pestered by her parents and six siblings.

Joe Restoule General

Joe is an Anishnaabe from the Dokis First Nation. He enjoys his life as an elementary school teacher at the Six Nations of the Grand River First Nation where he resides with his wife Aisha and their daughter Carrara. He attended the University of Windsor for his Honours BA, Queen's University for his B. Ed. and the University of Western Ontario for his M. Ed. His past exploits in media include stints as an award-winning talk radio DJ/host and independent newspaper writer. He hopes to one day publish a book about the teaching profession.

Sara General

Sara is from the Six Nations of the Grand River, and was a student at McMaster University, Ohsweken, ON when she submitted her story *Going the Distance* in 2006 to the Our Story Challenge. Her story won third place in the 19-29 age category.

Tony Liske

Tony is a full Dene Dogrib and a member of Dene First Nation. His grandfather is Antoine Liske and his grandmother is Elise Liske. His grandparents raised Liske in the culture and tradition of the Dene Dogrib. He claims this important heritage is a major part of his identity and will be passed on through the generations, to his children's children.

Nicole Munro
Nicole is from the Siksika Nation in Alberta and she is currently in her graduating year. From the time she was young, she was inspired to read books on her own after having her mother read to her. Inevitably, reading spurred an interest in writing and she hopes to become an author. She loves to read books and manga (Japanese comics) and enjoys writing stories. She counts J.R.R. Tolkien, Bill Myers, Frank Peretti, C.S. Lewis, and Watsuki Nobuhiro (manga artist/writer) among her favourite authors, and some favourite books include *The Outsiders* (S.E. Hinton), *The Lord of the Flies* (William Golding), and *Star Wars: Revenge of the Sith* (Matthew Stover).

Nicholas Printup
Nicholas was in Grade 12, attending Lakeshore High School in Ridgeway, Ontario when he submitted his story *A Day of Healing* in 2005 to the Our Story Challenge.

Trisha Redman
Trisha emphasises her story, *Makya*, reaches beyond Native history and explores the difficulty faced by two cultures when they first meet. She notes that throughout history – from Adolf Hitler's domination over Europe during the Second World War, to Canada's use of Chinese labourers to build the Canadian Pacific Railway, and to modern conflicts in the Middle East – all people can be cruel to each other regardless of race. Trisha grew up in Armstrong, British Columbia and enjoyed baseball, dance, and participated in the Armstrong 4-H swine club. In 2005, she graduated from Pleasant Valley High School.

Sable Sweetgrass
Sable is a single mother to her three-year-old boy, Zachary. She is from the Kainai Nation and lives in Calgary. Sable says she wrote her first story while serving detention in Grade six and hasn't stopped writing since. She thanks her mom, Molly Wells, and grandma, Sikotan (Mary Sweetgrass) "for absolutely everything." Currently, Sable is finishing a bachelor's degree in English at the University of Calgary, as well as studying international Indigenous studies and film. She made her first short digital film last year, *Nitsitapiima* (Family), and is the president of the Calgary Aboriginal Arts Awareness Society.

Caitlyn Therrien
Caitlyn was born in New Westminster, British Columbia. A recent high school graduate, Caitlyn aspires to become a professional opera singer. As the child of a First Nation family, she says she takes deep pride in her culture and cherishes the traditional name she was given, Wz-Ws-Kas, which means 'Little Robin: caller of the rain.' Caitlyn currently lives in Port Coquitlam, British Columbia.

Amanda Wapass-Griffin
Amanda is from Thunderchild First Nation in Saskatchewan, Treaty 6 Territory. At the University of Saskatchewan Amanda discovered her passion: Native studies. There, she explored the rich history of her ancestors and the cultural aspects of being Aboriginal, graduating with a bachelor of education degree. Amanda facilitates Aboriginal Awareness Education workshops – a job she says enables her to make the history of her people come alive for others, break down misconceptions about Aboriginal People that exist in Canada today and build bridges of understanding.

Denise Marie Williams
Born and raised in Ladysmith, British Columbia, Denise feels she has been rooted in a place full of tradition and natural beauty. She has pride in her heritage and works passionately in her role with Indian and Northern Affairs Canada in an effort to be part of the advancement of local First Nations communities. She plans to complete her degree in environmental sciences within the next year and aspires to address environmental issues on First Nations land. Denise currently resides in Port Coquitlam, British Columbia with her wonderful, supportive partner, Jourdain.

Kyle G. Wilson
Kyle is from Gitxsan Nation in BC, he was a student at Hazelton Secondary in New Hazelton, BC when he submitted his story *The Power of One and All* in 2006 to the Our Story Challenge. His story won third place in the 14-18 age category.

Jessica Yarrow
Jessica lives in Belleville, Ontario with her parents and sister. She graduated from Centennial Secondary School with Ontario Scholar status and in September 2006 entered Queen's University in Kingston. Jessica is working toward a bachelor of music with plans to attain a master's degree in music therapy – the creative and therapeutic use of music to heal the body and soul. She often performs at music festivals, in musicals and for elderly or palliative patients. The Our Story Writing Challenge was her first attempt at short story writing beyond her high school classroom experience. Along with writing, Jessica also enjoys jewellery making and creating custom purses for clients from unique and recyclable materials such as candy wrappers. Her fascination with Aboriginal culture has drawn her to research and learn more about Aboriginal history.

Marilyn Dumont
Her first collection, *A Really Good Brown Girl*, won the 1997 Gerald Lampert Memorial Award from the League of Canadian Poets. This collection is now in its tenth printing, and selections from it are widely anthologized in secondary and post-secondary literature texts. Her second collection, *green girl dreams Mountains*, won the 2001 Stephan G. Stephansson Award from the Writers Guild of Alberta. Marilyn has been the writer in residence at the universities of Alberta, Windsor and Toronto and at Grant MacEwan College in Edmonton. She teaches creative writing through Athabasca University and was a mentor for the 2006 Wired Writing Program at the Banff Centre for the Arts. Marilyn continues to work on a fourth manuscript in which she explores Métis history, politics and identity through her ancestral figure, Gabriel Dumont.